WAS SHE JUST A...

FALL GIRL?

Trouble comes in bright packages. Like Velda.

Jim Horton knew she was trouble the minute he saw her. Maybe it was the way she swung her body when she walked. Or maybe it was the way she ran that little red tongue around her lips when she looked at him.

And maybe it was the way she flirted with other men in front of her husband—as if he weren't even there—*as if he were already dead...*

MYSTERIES BY RICHARD DEMING

THE MANVILLE MOON SERIES

The Gallows in My Garden
Tweak the Devil's Nose
Give the Girl a Gun

OTHER NOVELS

Anything But Saintly
Body for Sale
Death of a Pusher
Edge of the Law
Fall Girl
Hit and Run
She'll HAte Me Tomorrow
This Game of Murder
Vice Cop

FALL GIRL

RICHARD DEMING

WILDSIDE PRESS

for Birch

Published by Wildside Press LLC.
www.wildsidebooks.com

CHAPTER I

The tall man signed the registration card with a flourish, then examined the signature, "James Horton," with satisfaction. It was a pleasant experience to be using his own name in a strange town.

The girl behind the hotel desk picked up the card, entered the room number 414, and glanced up at him with what started out to be an impersonal smile. As often happened when women took their first thorough look at him, the smile didn't remain impersonal. It broadened into a surprised grin of real welcome.

James Horton was used to this reaction, though he had never quite understood it. While he had a pleasant enough face, he wasn't at all handsome in the conventional meaning of the word. For one thing his broad, wide-nosed face was splashed with freckles. For another his coarse, sandy hair was so resistant to comb-and-brush discipline, he had given up the battle and wore it in a quarter-inch crew cut. For a third, his ears stuck out. But he was six feet three with unnaturally wide shoulders and a slim waist, and that alone was enough to make most women look twice.

The girl asked, "Will you be staying with us long, Mr. Horton?"

He studied her for a moment before answering. She was an attractive redhead with clear, milky skin and wide-spaced green eyes. In deference to the Hotel Lawford's conservative atmosphere, she wore a severely-tailored gray suit, but it failed to conceal that she had a body designed to be shown off in low-cut evening gowns. He guessed her age at about twenty-five, five years younger than he was. She looked as though she might be worth cultivating.

With a pleasant smile, he said, "I'm not sure, miss. Depends on how soon I find a permanent place to live."

"Oh, you're moving to Rice City?" she inquired.

"Just as a summer resident," he said. "Hope to buy a home along the beach. I have an appointment with a real-estate man tomorrow to look at some places."

"Well, we'll certainly be glad to have you here," the girl said. Then, realizing there was an unnecessary amount of enthusiasm in her voice, she blushed.

To cover her confusion, she looked toward the bell captain's desk and called, "Front!"

A bell-hop came over and picked up Horton's bags.

* * * *

It was nine o'clock, Friday morning on June sixth when James Horton checked into the Hotel Lawford. By ten he had showered and changed to a freshly-pressed suit, and had descended to the lobby again.

He was on his way to the front door when a startled feminine voice called, "Jim Horton!"

Stopping, he turned to see a woman approaching him from the door of the coffee shop a few yards away. She was a tall, perfectly-formed brunette in her late twenties with jet-black hair framing delicate features in a pageboy bob. She was dark, with full, sensuous lips and almond eyes which gave her a slightly oriental look.

He waited until she neared, gave her a warm but wary smile and said, "Hello, Belle."

She came to a halt a foot from him and examined him with a mixture of pleasure and speculation. "What in the world are you doing in Rice City?" she asked.

"Thinking of making it my summer home," he said. "I'll return the question. The colonel with you?"

She ignored the inquiry. "You staying here at the hotel?" she asked.

He nodded.

She touched the backs of fingers to her lips. "I'm sorry," she said. "I shouldn't have yelled your real name across the lobby like that."

Horton grinned. "Why not? It's the one on the register."

"Oh. You're not here on business then?" Her voice sounded relieved.

"Yeah, as a matter of fact. Legitimate business."

"You?" Belle asked with raised brows. "That I'll believe when the colonel starts giving to charity."

"Fact, Belle. Thinking of buying a home on the river and settling down to a life of fishing."

The speculative look returned to Belle's eyes. "A real estate deal, eh? Who's the mark?"

"I told you it's strictly legitimate," Horton said patiently. "I've retired."

She gave a disbelieving little chuckle. "Still as close-mouthed as ever, aren't you? Do you think the colonel and I would try to chisel in?" She added quickly, "Don't answer that."

Horton grinned at her.

Belle laid a hand on his arm. "Honestly, Jim, you know I wouldn't, even if the colonel wanted to. You don't have to pretend with me. Don't expect me to believe the top bunco artist in the profession is going legit."

He shrugged. "If it pleases you to think evil of your fellow man."

She dropped her hand from his arm. "Well, if you don't trust me—"

Horton interrupted dryly. "Where's the colonel?"

"Over at the Rafferty House. Only he's demoted himself for the business at hand. He's Major Herbert Walsh, U.S. Army, retired."

Horton gave his head a reproving shake. "Can't you get him to drop the military titles, Belle? His M.O. sticks out like a chorus girl's bust after every score. He might as well use his own name."

"You know Colonel Bob," she said with a grin. "He's not happy unless he's playing the old soldier, prematurely put to pasture because of his honorable wounds. Incidentally, I'm Mrs. Belle Whitney here at the hotel. Room 727, in case you're interested."

Automatically he threw her an intimate smile. Belle gave a mock tremble.

"Don't do that," she said. "Even knowing you don't mean it, it gives me shivers."

"Maybe I do mean it," he said. "You know why I've always steered clear of you."

"The story was that the colonel's a friend of yours," she said petulantly. "And you don't encroach on friends' territories. But you must know by now that my relationship with Colonel Bob is strictly business. I always thought you just didn't want to waste your talent on a colleague. Professional ethics would make it repugnant to you to skip with my life savings after you'd made me fall madly in love with you."

He frowned at her. "Hey, that's not fair. When did I ever cheat a woman by making love to her?"

"I guess it was below the belt," she admitted. "You usually only take them as ask for it. But did it ever occur to you that you can cheat a woman by *not* making love to her?"

Horton grinned. "Maybe I'm afraid you'd abscond with *my* life savings."

"Take a chance," she urged. "Try living dangerously."

"Perhaps I will sometime," he said non-committally. "Maybe I'll ring you."

"Room 727. And don't forget the name. Mrs. Belle Whitney."

"Sure, Belle. I'll remember."

With a smile of good-by, he moved on toward the street door.

He hadn't asked what sort of con game Belle Jarvis and "Colonel" Robert Desmond were planning to pull on some unsuspecting Rice City mark. Not because he didn't have a natural curiosity. He just knew it would have done no more good to ask than it had done Belle to inquire about his plans.

CHAPTER II

At a car-rental agency Horton rented a 1958 Plymouth Belvedere for the day. He spent the rest of the morning examining the town.

Rice City had a population of nearly a half million. From his study of Chamber of Commerce material, Horton knew that it had a diversity of small industry, but no large industrial plants. It was an attractive city, without much great wealth, but without much slum area either. It was a city of neat, middle-income homes in the outlying areas and neat, moderate-rental apartment houses in the downtown area. There were a few downtown streets near the riverfront where tenement houses looked a little run-down, shops were a trifle shabby and taverns catered to an overalled clientele, but on the whole, it seemed to be a clean, well-ordered community.

The surface appearance was a fraud, Horton knew. He hadn't blindly picked Rice City for his present operation. Before choosing it, he had done careful research on a dozen communities of similar size. He had deliberately selected Rice City because it had the sort of police department which could be counted on to mistreat arrested out-of-towners, or anyone else, for that matter, who was not in on the local fix. He meant to get himself arrested, and to endure as much mistreatment as he could heckle the police into giving him.

The summer-home area lay north of the town along the river's edge. Here the bank was dotted by cottages and homes which grew progressively larger and more expensive the farther they got from the hub of town.

Horton stopped for a time in a small park perched atop the river bluff, and took in the view. Extending from both sides of the park, brightly-painted cottages lined the base of the bluff. A wide sand beach ran as far as he could see in both directions. Numerous people in swimming suits lay in the early June sun, or splashed in the clear, slowly-moving water of Rice River. A number of fishermen trolled from boats with outboard motors. A half-dozen sails glistened whitely in the sunshine.

Horton sighed. It was such a pleasant scene, he almost wished he really meant to buy one of the beach homes the Acme Realty Company thought it was going to show him the next day. Driving back to the downtown area, he found a public phone and from the yellow pages of the phone book he made a list of all the used-car lots in the center of town. He then proceeded to make a careful check of the lots.

He didn't stop at any of them. He merely drove slowly past each, eyeing the cars lined up on display.

On the eighth lot he passed, he was gratified to spot a 1955 Jaguar. He checked the huge sign over the entrance to the lot. It read: HONEST JOHN QUINCY'S USED CARS. LOWEST PRICES, HIGHEST TRADE-INS, EASIEST TERMS IN TOWN.

He drove past another half-dozen used-car lots before he was satisfied that there probably wasn't another used Jaguar in town. There were few sports cars of any make on the lots, as a matter of fact, and he saw none driving the streets. Rice City wasn't a sports car town.

He picked one other lot as the place to start his operation. A billboard on its street side announced that it was run by TRUSTING JOE GANNON, and that it too offered the lowest prices, highest trade-ins and easiest terms in town. Horton picked it because it didn't have a single sports car on display.

By now it was past noon. He stopped for lunch at a small café, then drove to the Rice City National Bank.

Horton encountered no difficulty in getting in to see the bank president. He merely mentioned to the president's secretary that he wished to open a couple of accounts and also discuss a mortgage loan. He was shown in at once.

Hanford Maytum, President of Rice City National, was a plump, balding man of fifty with the benign manner of Friar Tuck. He shook Horton's hand with reserved enthusiasm and asked him to have a seat.

"You wished to discuss a mortgage loan, Mr. Horton?" he asked, tactfully not mentioning the accounts Horton had told his secretary he wished to open.

"First things first," Horton said with a genial smile. "I'd like to open a couple of accounts before we talk business."

"Certainly, Mr. Horton. Interest or checking?"

"One of each," Horton said. "I'd like to put five thousand in the checking account and ten thousand in savings."

He handed Maytum a certified check for fifteen thousand dollars drawn on a St. Louis bank.

"Fine, Mr. Horton, fine," the bank president said. He examined the check, pressed a buzzer and handed the check back. "If you'll just endorse it, I'll have my secretary set up the accounts right away. You prefer the personalized checking account, or the regular?"

"By personalized, you mean with my name printed on the checks?"

"Yes, sir. Only thing is, we wouldn't be able to give you a check book before Monday. They have to be printed, you see."

"Then I'd better settle for the regular account," Horton decided. "I planned to buy a used car tomorrow."

The secretary entered in answer to Hanford Maytum's buzz. The bank president gave her instructions on setting up the two accounts. Horton endorsed the check and handed it to her. When the girl had gone out again, Maytum said, "Now what was it about the mortgage?"

"Well, I'm planning on establishing a summer home here, Mr. Maytum. My work permits me pretty free summers, and the fishing and boating available in your community appeals to me. My investment business in St. Louis will keep me there during the winter months, of course, but I mean to live here during most of June, July, and August."

Maytum nodded understandingly.

"I've been in correspondence with the Acme Realty Company," Horton went on. "Know it?"

Maytum nodded again. "Highly reputable firm. Keep their account here."

"Well, they know the type of beach home I wish. Nothing too elaborate. Something in about the twenty-thousand-dollar class. I have an appointment with a Mr. Weller over there to see some places tomorrow."

"I see. I know Weller. Very wide-awake real-estate man."

"If I find the place I want, I plan to make a down payment of ten thousand and finance the balance on a five-year mortgage."

Maytum smiled benignly. "That will be easy enough, I'm sure, Mr. Horton. Just drop in to see us when you're ready to sign the papers. And if there's any way we can be of service meanwhile, don't hesitate to ask."

"There is one minor way, as a matter of fact, Mr. Maytum. As I said, I plan to pick up a used car tomorrow. Can you recommend a reputable dealer?"

"Why, I believe all our local merchants are reputable," Maytum said cautiously.

"What I had in mind was a Jaguar," Horton said. He gave the banker a sheepish smile. "My sole vice."

"What's that?"

"Sports cars. I'm rather a nut on the subject. Rarely drive anything else. The Jaguar's my favorite."

Maytum smiled. "Afraid you won't find many sports cars in Rice City, Mr. Horton. It's a pretty conservative town. Offhand, I can't think of a lot where you might find a Jaguar."

Horton stood up. "Well, I'll just have to look around. Thanks for your time, Mr. Maytum. It was nice meeting you."

Maytum rose too and shook hands. "My pleasure, Mr. Horton. Just see the girl on the way out. She should have your accounts ready by now."

A few moments later Horton walked out of the bank with a bank book and check book in his pocket. He was well pleased with the way things had gone. Hanford Maytum would make an excellent witness for the plaintiff, if he remembered the details of their conversation.

It would have been inconvenient if he had happened to know where a Jaguar was for sale, but fortunately he hadn't.

Having no more immediate use for a car, Horton returned the Plymouth to the rental agency. He spent the rest of the afternoon at a movie. He got back to the Hotel Lawford shortly before six.

The red-haired girl was still on duty at the desk, he noticed as he crossed the lobby. It suddenly occurred to him that he had no plans at all for the evening, and that the girl might make a pleasant dinner companion. He started toward the desk, then changed his mind when three arriving guests suddenly converged on the girl at the same time, all wanting to register.

Horton decided to give her ten minutes to dispose of the new guests, then phone her from his room.

At five after six he lifted his phone and said, "Desk, please."

After a moment's wait, a man's voice said, "Front desk."

"This is four fourteen," Horton said. "May I speak to the red-haired girl who works the desk? I don't know her name."

"Sorry, Mr.—" There was a pause, obviously during which the man glanced at a room chart. "—Horton. She goes off duty at six. May I help you?"

"Thanks, but it isn't important," Horton said.

The man might have mentioned her name, he thought, mildly irked that he hadn't. He was surprised to realize he was deeply disappointed at missing the girl. The prospect of dining alone suddenly loomed bleakly.

He started to reach for the phone again to call room 727, then halted the movement. He was in no mood to settle for second choice.

Instead he stripped, took his second shower of the day, carefully redressed and descended for a lonely dinner.

CHAPTER III

The hotel dining room was only about half full. Horton paused in the doorway and glanced around as he waited for the headwaiter to move toward him.

At a table a short distance from the entrance he saw Belle Jarvis seated across from a plump, pompous-looking man of about fifty. Horton thought ruefully that apparently he would have been out of luck even if he had been willing to settle for second choice.

The headwaiter was before him then, murmuring a polite, "Good evening, sir."

"Just a single, please," Horton said. Then, on an impish impulse, he pointed to the table immediately behind Belle's and asked, "Is that table taken?"

"No, sir," the headwaiter said, and led him over to it.

Belle's back was to the door. When Horton seated himself facing her back, she was unaware of it.

A waitress brought water and a menu. Horton ordered a dry martini, opened the menu as the girl moved away, and strained to hear what Belle and her companion were saying while he studied it.

He wasn't in the least ashamed of eavesdropping. He assumed the man with Belle was the mark she and the colonel were setting up for a score, and it was accepted professional ethics among the exclusive fraternity to which he belonged to attempt to learn rival colleagues' plans by any means which would not spoil the game. Neither Belle nor Colonel Robert Desmond would hesitate for an instant to tap his phone or steam open his mail, if they thought such prying would give them an opportunity to move in on his plans for a share of the profit.

Horton wasn't interested in moving in on their plans, for he always operated alone. He was eavesdropping merely because custom gave him the moral right to do it, and he was bored.

Belle was saying, "It's so hard for a woman with no business knowledge to know what to do, Mr. Tyrell. When my husband was alive, he handled all our investments, so I really know nothing about the stock market." She emitted a tinkling little laugh. "If the major didn't watch me like a hawk, I suppose some unscrupulous broker would have plucked me long ago."

The plump man nodded understandingly. "One sure safeguard against that, Mrs. Winters. Invest in government bonds."

"Oh, I *have* those," Belle said. "I wouldn't dream of touching my savings." She laughed again. "Major Walsh wouldn't let me anyway. The old dear treats me rather like an idiot child. But I want this ten thousand from the sale of my home to work for me. My husband always said part of your money should be in gilt-edged securities, and the rest should be invested to make more, even if it involved a calculated risk. But George had such good business sense, and I don't have a bit."

"The stock market's a little beyond me," Tyrell said. "I own a few shares of G.M. and a bit of TV stock. But long as I can make money manufacturing boxes, I'll leave market speculation to the other fellow. Afraid I'm not going to be much help."

Belle reached across the table to squeeze her companion's hand. "You have such a fund of common sense, though, Mr. Tyrell. I'm sure I can rely on your judgment."

Mr. Tyrell inflated a little. "I'm not one to be taken in very easily," he admitted. "But don't you trust this fellow?"

Belle emitted her tinkling little laugh again. "Major Walsh? Why, of course. He was my husband's best friend. And he's practically a father to me."

"Oh. Don't you think he knows his stocks, then?"

"The major would probably challenge you to a duel if he heard that," Belle said with a smile. "Haven't you ever heard of Major Herbert Walsh?"

Tyrell shook his head. "Should I have?"

"Well, he's considered one of the outstanding authorities on the stock market in the country. It's just a hobby, you know. He was a career soldier until the Korean War, and then he was seriously wounded and discharged. He never plays the market himself. He just enjoys studying it. Some of his friends have made fortunes from his advice, but he himself has never made a nickel. Doesn't believe in speculation. He's let me make a few dollars, but not nearly as much as I could have if he wasn't so conservative. He never gives me a tip unless he's convinced it's sure-fire."

The plump man frowned puzzledly. "Don't see why you need my opinion then."

"You don't understand," Belle told him. "I can never make head or tail of what the major's talking about when he gets on the subject of stocks. He's so full of expressions like money markets, and bullish trends, he might as well be speaking Swahili for all the sense I can make out of it. I need you to act as a sort of interpreter."

Tyrell gave her an indulgent smile. "I guess I know enough about economics to do that, if that's all you want."

The waitress brought Horton's cocktail then, and he lost track of the conversation while he was ordering dinner. He really didn't have to hear any more to diagnose the plot, though. It was merely a variation of the ancient gimmick of the supposedly rich widow flattering the mark by asking his advice on an investment. Shortly the colonel would be along with such a sure-fire market tip, the mark would begin to wonder if he might get in on the deal too.

The colonel would be a little dubious about letting a stranger in on such a sure thing, but after some coaxing by Belle and a promise of secrecy from the mark, he would let himself be brought around.

By the time Horton's dinner arrived, Belle and Tyrell were almost finished with their coffee. It was no surprise to Horton when Colonel Bob Desmond appeared just as Belle and the mark were getting ready to leave the table.

The colonel was a portly man of sixty with a florid face, bright, bird-like eyes and a ragged mustache of sandy color. He had equally ragged eyebrows of the same hue, which suggested his hair had once been that shade too. There was no other way to tell, because he was totally bald.

There was an odd mixture of Britishness and Americanism about the colonel. Physically he had all the attributes of the stock British colonial officer. A habit of hiking his left eyebrow at the same time he squinted his right eye even created the effect that he wore an invisible monocle. But his manner was that of an American officer. His bearing was erect without being stiff, his speech crisp, and he studded his conversation with military expressions.

Horton happened to know he had never served a day in any army.

The colonel was passing his table when Horton looked up at him calmly. The colonel's gaze was on Belle and her companion, but the movement of Horton's head caused him to glance sidewise. His mouth popped open.

Without a sign of recognition, Horton returned his attention to his steak. The colonel recovered and moved on.

When he reached Belle's table, Colonel Bob inclined his body in the barest suggestion of a bow, said, "Ah, there you are, my dear," and looked inquiringly at Belle's companion.

Belle performed introductions, referring to the colonel as "Major Walsh." As Tyrell started to rise, Colonel Bob waved him back to his seat.

"At ease, sir," he said. "Make it a rule myself never to stand except for ladies and the Star-Spangled Banner. Silly convention. Meet so many people, you'd be bobbing up and down all the time if you didn't establish and hold a position."

Tyrell sat down again and caught Belle's eye. Major Walsh was a pompous old bear, her look seemed to say, but rather a family pet, and she hoped Tyrell would be forbearing with him.

Tyrell was obviously flattered. Probably he had been prepared to be a little in awe of the stock-market wizard. But Belle's tacit invitation changed his attitude to one of indulgence.

Horton knew how things would develop from there. You aren't likely to be wary of a man you condescend to. And when your condescension is tinged with genuine liking, you are even less inclined to be wary of him.

Everybody liked Colonel Bob. Except in retrospect, after he had faded out of town.

Tyrell said, "Sit down, Major, and we'll order more coffee."

The colonel's eyes flicked sidewise at Horton's table in a movement missed by Tyrell, but caught by Belle. He said, "If you've finished, why don't we all make an advance on the cocktail lounge?"

Belle instantly rose and said, "That would be nice. I'd like a brandy."

Casually she glanced around, and her eyes widened when she saw Horton seated immediately behind her. Raising her chin in a gesture of disapproval, she swept by his table without looking at him.

She hadn't even given Tyrell time to pay the bill. As the colonel followed Belle toward the cocktail lounge, the plump man signed his check and dropped a tip on the table. Then he followed.

Later, as Horton left the dining room, he glanced through the open door of the cocktail lounge. The three of them were seated at a table in front of the empty fireplace. The colonel was speaking, while Belle and the plump box manufacturer listened with rapt attention.

* * * *

At ten-thirty that night, Horton was reading in his room in his shirt-sleeves. A soft rap came at the door.

Laying aside his book, he rose and opened the door. He wasn't overly surprised to find Belle in the hall.

"Evening, Peeping Tom," she said. "Alone?"

"Uh-huh," he said, and stepped aside for her to enter.

She advanced to the center of the room and glanced around with the womanly air of searching for some sign of bachelor disorder. She seemed disappointed at not finding any. Horton pushed the door shut.

"Sorry I have nothing to drink," he said. "I could phone room service."

"Never mind," she said. "I'll settle for a cigarette."

He crossed to his dresser, picked up a pack and offered it. She selected a cigarette and waited while he held flame to it. She inhaled deeply, blew smoke from her nostrils, and studied him from narrowed eyes.

He examined her in return. She was lovely in a green evening gown which left her dark-skinned shoulders bare and dipped in a deep V to expose the upper swell of perfect breasts.

"Sit down?" he asked.

"No, thanks. I'll only be a minute."

He raised his eyebrows.

"I came to give you a tip," she said.

"Yeah?"

"Don't take a fall in this town, Jim."

"I wasn't planning to," he said. "But why not?"

"They throw the book at you. They hand out hard time like they own the calendar."

Horton raised his brows. "I understood it was pretty wide-open."

"Sure, for the locals. They've got the fix in. This character Tony Manzetti, who has his fingers in all the local rackets, has the chief of police and the D.A. right in his pocket. Which is why they're so heavy on outsiders. There have been so many rumbles about corruption in the papers, the police and the D.A. try to make it look as though they're doing their jobs when they get hold of a lawbreaker who isn't protected by the machine."

Horton said, "Sounds logical."

"Another thing. Steer clear of a local named Honest John Quincy."

"Why?" he asked, remembering that this was the name of the used car dealer with the Jaguar. "That your mark?"

"He started out to be," she said candidly. "Until we found out who he was. Then we dropped him like a hot potato."

"Oh? Why?"

"He's chairman of the Civic Crime Committee, a volunteer organization of businessmen and community leaders dedicated to the elimination of rackets in Rice City. They haven't had much luck in fighting the Manzetti machine, so they take out their frustration on minor criminals. If you get picked up for anything at all here more serious than a traffic charge, Honest John will be breathing down the D.A.'s neck to see that justice is done."

"If things are so rough," he asked, "why did you and the colonel pick Rice City?"

"You have to go where the marks are," Belle shrugged.

"They're everywhere."

Horton eyed the girl speculatively for a moment and then grinned. "You didn't have to tell me all that you know," he said. "You don't need a reason to visit."

"What are you talking about?"

"Do you want me to be brutally frank?"

She raised her chin. "You usually are."

"You just wanted an excuse," he said.

"Excuse for what?"

"To come to my room," he said in a mocking tone.

CHAPTER IV

Belle's chin went higher and her eyes blazed. Crossing to the dresser, she ground out her cigarette with a vicious gesture and wordlessly started for the door. Horton had moved too, though, and his back was to it.

"Get out of my way, you beast!" she said.

He gave her a lazy smile. "You're pretty when you're mad, sugar."

"I said, get out of my way!"

Instead of answering, he took her by the shoulders and slowly drew her against his chest. He was not smiling now. She made no resistance, but her body was passive.

He held her quietly, looking down into her upturned face.

"I'm glad you're here," he said.

One of his hands left her bare shoulder and his fingers wound into her dark hair. Brutally he jerked her head back until her face pointed straight upward. He kissed her savagely, forcing her lips apart. And then her arms slid about his neck and she strained against him eagerly.

When he finally raised his mouth from hers, her brusied lips remained parted. Her head was still forced backward by his grip on her hair, but she made no attempt to free herself.

He lifted her bodily, took three steps, and tossed her on the bed in a heap. She bounced to one elbow and stared at him with a mixture of fright and expectancy. He turned his back, walked to the doorway and snapped out the light.

In the darkness he heard her shoes drop to the floor, then the rustle of clothing. He waited by the doorway until the rustling ceased.

Then he moved toward the bed.

Just before he reached it, her voice said in a barely-audible whisper, "You may as well know it. It *was* just an excuse."

* * * *

Horton slept until nine. Sometime in the middle of the night Belle had left him. A parting kiss on his shoulder had momentarily roused him, but he had immediately fallen asleep again. He had a vague memory of her whispering, "Thanks, darling."

In the light of morning the words seemed unlikely, particularly the thanks. He decided he must have dreamed them.

Downstairs he stopped at the desk for a paper to read at breakfast. The red-haired girl was on duty again. He was about to mention his attempt to phone her for a dinner date when a headline in the paper he had just bought distracted him. It blared: CRIME COMMITTEE HEAD THREATENED.

Immediately beneath the headline was the photograph of a heavy-featured, black-browed man. The photograph was labeled: John Quincy.

Bemused, Horton walked away reading the item without saying to the girl what he had intended. It read:

> "Honest" John Quincy, local auto dealer and chairman of the Civic Crime Committee, reported to police last night that he had received a threat against his life. The threat was in the form of a note composed of words clipped from a newspaper and pasted onto a sheet of paper. It read: "Call off your dogs, snooper, or you're done. This is your last warning. Next you get a bullet."
>
> According to Quincy, the note was left in his residence mailbox, at 223 River Road, sometime after the eleven A.M. mail delivery. The box was not checked again until eight P.M., when the threatening note was discovered.
>
> In an exclusive interview with a representative of this paper, Quincy expressed the belief that the threat referred to his committee's recent probing into local rackets.
>
> "This is but another instance of the arrogance of Rice City's organized criminal element," he said in a prepared statement. "When known racketeers have the gall to threaten death to any law-abiding citizen who presumes to question their right to run roughshod over a community of a half-million people, it is time to examine our entire local political apparatus. What gives these racketeers such outrageous confidence in their power? Thinking citizens might well ask if the apparent immunity to the law enjoyed by certain racketeers in control of Rice City doesn't indicate a tie-in with the politicians in power, or even with the police. I have this to say in answer to this brazen threat: If anyone, including a certain gentleman named Manzetti, thinks such a threat can deter me from my battle against organized lawlessness, they have tried to intimidate the wrong man."
>
> Presumably Quincy's reference was to political boss and alleged racketeer Antonio (The Boss) Manzetti, whose affairs have been under investigation by the Civic Crime Committee for some time.
>
> Manzetti could not be reached for comment.

Horton mused over the item all during breakfast. He had picked quite a town, he decided. Either Quincy's Crime Committee was closer to breaking the local rackets than Belle had seemed to think, or this

Manzetti man was so powerfully entrenched, he was totally contemptuous of what the public thought. For if the threat had originated with Manzetti, as Quincy seemed to believe, it was either a measure of desperation or a brazen flaunting of power.

In either event, Horton thought with a grin, it ought to put Honest John Quincy in the proper mood to be highly intolerant of any sort of lawbreaking. This was going to make his own setup sure fire.

* * * *

It was eleven A.M. when Horton arrived at Trusting Joe Gannon's Used-Car Lot. As soon as he set foot on it, a young man wearing a conservative blue suit stepped from the office building and approached him.

"Help you, sir?" he asked with a friendly smile.

"I was looking for a sports car," Horton said, glancing up and down the rows of automobiles. "Don't see any on display."

The young man chuckled. "Not in Rice City, mister. People here just don't go for sports cars. We have a fine selection of hard-tops, though. Next best thing."

"Well, I really wanted a sports car," Horton said. "Happen to know any lot that has one for sale?"

The young salesman shook his head, faintly amused at the suggestion that he might recommend some competitor's lot. "You won't find one in town, mister. They're a drug on the market. We ship them to the west coast fast as we get them. They go like hotcakes there. Here we never even put them on display. Let me show you what we have got."

With a show of reluctance, Horton allowed himself to be shown the hard-top convertibles on the lot. He expressed mild interest in a 1958 Mercury with only nine thousand miles on it.

Encouraged by this nibble, the salesman moved into high gear. Ten minutes later, after coming down three hundred dollars from the first asking price of twenty-four-hundred, he got Horton to agree to buy the car.

The young man let out a satisfied sigh. "Just step into the office and we'll make out the papers," he said. "How do you want to finance it?"

"I don't," Horton told him. "I'll pay cash. You'll accept a personal check, won't you?"

The salesman looked a little dubious. "I don't know about that, sir. The banks aren't open on Saturday, and usually we don't accept checks unless they are. So we can phone and verify the account, you see."

Horton shrugged. "In that case I'll try another lot."

"No, no," the young man said hurriedly. "I'm sure we'll be able to work it out. Only thing is, you'll have to talk to the boss."

He escorted Horton into the office and introduced him to Trusting Joe Gannon. The proprietor was a thin, balding man of middle age with an affable manner.

When Gannon learned that Horton was not a local resident, he, too, seemed dubious about accepting a check. Nevertheless he decided to do it.

He really didn't have much choice. In the first place Horton possessed more than his share of the bunco artist's stock in trade: an ability to charm strangers into trusting him on sight. In the second place Horton had highly convincing credentials.

He explained to Gannon his reason for being in town, and displayed a letter from the Acme Realty Company confirming an appointment to show him some beach homes that afternoon. He showed his bank book and mentioned bank president Hanford Maytum by name.

In the third place Trusting Joe Gannon was confronted with the choice of either accepting the check or losing the sale, for Horton made it clear that if the check wasn't acceptable, he would find some other dealer who was willing to take the risk.

In the end Trusting Joe lived up to his name. He accepted the check, stipulating only that Horton write his hotel and room number on the back.

At five minutes after noon Horton drove the Mercury off the lot.

CHAPTER V

Horton drove the Mercury only six blocks. He took it straight to Honest John Quincy's Used-Car Lot. He parked alongside the small office building in the center of the lot, got out of the car, and waited. He was pleased to note that the Jaguar still stood on the lot.

When no salesman appeared after several moments, he stepped to the door of the building and peered through the glass pane of the door. The door led into a small office containing a desk and a couple of tables, a few chairs and a filing cabinet. The office took up only half the building, and two doors on its inside wall led to rooms in the other half.

A man and a woman were in the office, apparently in heated argument. The man was in his fifties, heavy-set, with black hair beginning to gray and thick black brows. Horton recognized him from his newspaper picture as Honest John Quincy. The woman was a stunning blonde of about thirty.

The boss exercising the ancient prerogative of bawling out the hired help, Horton decided. He bounced his knuckles on the glass to alert them to his presence, opened the door and entered.

Both the man and woman looked at him. Quincy's face was dark with anger. With an effort he smoothed his features and managed a strained smile. The blonde at first stared at him sulkily. Then Horton smiled at her, and her sulkiness evaporated. She studied him with open interest.

Quincy said, "Yes, sir?"

"Looking for a salesman," Horton said.

"They're both out to lunch at the moment," Quincy told him. "I'm the owner. Can I help you?"

"Maybe. I'm interested in that Jaguar you have outside."

Growing conscious of the woman's gaze still on him, Horton glanced at her. She was looking him up and down with no attempt to disguise her deliberate examination. Accepting the challenge, he stared back at her with equal deliberation.

She was a lovely thing, as cool and crisp as a fresh salad, with perfect features and a slim, rounded body. She wore a white linen dress with a design of red flowers, open-toed white pumps and no stockings, so that flaming red toenails were exposed. From the way the dress clung Horton suspected she wore nothing under it.

Horton returned his attention to Quincy when the man said in a suddenly sharp voice, "I'll be glad to show it to you."

An instant later Horton understood what had caused the man's tone to sharpen. The woman said in a soft drawl, "Why don't you ask the gentleman his name, dear? And introduce us."

Horton glanced at her again, this time noting the wedding ring she wore. She wasn't an employee after all, he realized, but Quincy's wife. And they had been looking each other over right in front of her husband.

Quincy scowled at the woman. When he made no attempt to take her suggestion, she gave Horton an intimate smile and said, "I'm Velda Quincy."

"James Horton," he said with a formal nod. "How do you do?"

Then he turned abruptly and opened the door, glancing over his shoulder at Quincy. He had no intention of getting caught in the middle of a family argument. Quincy sullenly followed him outside.

They had barely reached the Jaguar when Velda Quincy came from the building, too. Walking over to them, she said to her husband, "You forgot to give me the money, dear."

All the time she was approaching, and even while she spoke, her eyes were on Horton.

Quincy started to say with suppressed fury, "I told you—" Then he broke it off, reached for his wallet and slapped a number of bills into her outstretched palm. Horton noted that the back of his thick neck was fire-red.

The woman thrust the bills into her purse without glancing at them, and gave Horton a smile of good-by. "Nice to have met you, Mr. Horton," she said in her soft drawl. "Perhaps we'll meet again."

"My pleasure, Mrs. Quincy," Horton said politely, ignoring her second sentence.

From the corner of his eye, he watched the sway of her hips as she walked to a red Chrysler convertible parked near the office building. She had to drive past the Jaguar to get off the lot, and she threw him a final intimate smile as she passed.

Horton, aware that her husband's gaze was on him, merely gave her a distant nod.

Once the woman was out of sight, both he and Quincy were able to return their minds to business. Horton listened attentively as Quincy extolled the virtues of the Jaguar.

He wanted three thousand dollars for it.

Horton had a fair knowledge of sport cars. A 1955 Jaguar in good condition retailed for around two thousand. This one had thirty thousand miles on its speedometer, and there were several rust spots on its body. It was worth perhaps fifteen hundred.

"Is that the best you can do?" he asked.

"That's a rock-bottom price," Quincy assured him. "You won't find another Jaguar in town at that price."

Apparently the chairman of the Civic Crime Committee's aversion to rackets didn't include rackets legally classed as business operations.

Horton asked, "What'll you give me on my Mercury?"

Quincy walked over to the Mercury, glanced at the speedometer, then circled the car.

"Twelve hundred," he offered.

"That doesn't seem like very much," Horton said dubiously.

"Well, I might go to thirteen."

Horton said tentatively, "I thought maybe it would bring up to fifteen."

Quincy shook his head. "Out of the question. I'm cutting my profit to the bone now."

"Would you go fourteen?"

"Make it thirteen-fifty," Quincy said. "But that's absolutely the last word."

Horton said, "You've got a deal."

Quincy totally recovered from his spat with his wife. "You drive a hard bargain," he said with a rueful shake of his head. "The Jaguar's yours for a balance of sixteen-fifty."

Horton pulled out his check book and said in a diffident tone, "A check is all right, isn't it?"

Quincy frowned. "Personal?"

"Yes, sir." He added with a trace of overeagerness, "It's on a local bank. The Ritz City National. I mean the Rice City National."

"Um," Quincy said doubtfully. "Let's go inside and talk it over."

Back in the office Horton went full swing into his prepared act, deliberately calculated to make Quincy distrust him.

It was a sensitive performance. He did nothing as obvious as putting a furtive look on his face. It was essential that if at some future time Quincy had to testify from a witness stand, he would be unable truthfully to point out any specific remark or action on Horton's part which could logically be construed as guilty behavior. Horton merely acted a little too eager to close the deal and be on his way, and just frank enough to sound phony.

The climax came when Quincy examined his car registration and discovered that Horton had purchased the Mercury only that day. His eyes strayed to the phone on his desk.

Horton wanted to give him every opportunity to check with Trusting Joe Gannon. Glancing at his hands, he said, "Got a little dirty checking over the Jaguar. Have a washroom here?"

Quincy silently pointed to one of the two doors on the inside wall. His gaze followed Horton as he crossed the office and disappeared.

Inside the washroom Horton ran water hard for a moment, then softly stepped to the door and pressed his ear against it. He could hear the phone on Quincy's desk being dialed.

After a moment he heard Quincy's low-toned voice say, "Gannon? This is John Quincy."

There was a pause, then, "Think I've got a hot-check artist here, Joe. You sell a James Horton a Mercury today?"

After another pause, Quincy's startled voice said, "Less than a half-hour ago! For how much?"

A moment later he emitted a cynical little chuckle. "Well, well. He's trying to unload it on me for thirteen-fifty."

There was another, longer pause. Then Quincy said, "Of course he can't hear me. He's in the washroom. I'll stall him until you can get the police here. What? No, I'm all alone, so hurry. I don't much like his looks." His voice dropped even lower. "Hold it a sec, Joe. The door's opening."

The last remark puzzled Horton. He took his ear from the door and glanced at its edge to make certain he hadn't inadvertently caused it to crack open by leaning against it.

It was still tightly closed.

From the office there came a startled exclamation, followed by the thunderous explosion of a large-caliber gun. There was a stifled groan and the thud of a heavy body slumping to the floor.

CHAPTER VI

For a second or two, Horton was too startled to react. He heard the outer door of the office slam. Then he jerked open the washroom door.

At first glance the office seemed empty. He had to cross the room before he could see Quincy. The man had fallen from his chair behind his desk. He lay on his back making bubbling noises, and pink-flecked foam was dribbling from a corner of his mouth. A growing spot of blood was in the center of his chest.

Even as Horton bent over him, a rattling sound came from his throat and his eyes rolled sightlessly upward.

Horton grew conscious of the phone dangling from its cord just above the floor. He could hear Trusting Joe Gannon's excited voice squawking, "John! Was that a shot? John, what happened?"

Quietly he replaced the phone in its cradle.

Moving to the door, he opened it and glanced outside. No one was in sight who might have been the killer. Traffic was moving normally along the street. A middle-aged couple was walking along the sidewalk next to the lot. Another couple, younger, was looking into the window of a furniture store across the street. Half a block away a man sat on a bus-stop bench reading a newspaper. If any of them had heard the shot, apparently they had assumed it was a backfire.

Closing the door again, Horton did some furious thinking. It looked as though his fool-proof con game had suddenly developed into a fool-proof trap. With himself as the victim.

He considered his chances of convincing the police that he had nothing to do with the murder if he simply stood his ground and waited for them to arrive.

One item in his favor was that he had no gun. But perhaps the killer had tossed it somewhere in the lot for the police to find. If so, it might be difficult to convince them he wasn't the one who tossed it there.

Another item in his favor was that when the banks opened Monday, he could prove he hadn't been trying to cash hot checks. Then he realized this wouldn't be much of a defense. If his plan had worked out without being interrupted by murder, the investigation of him would have gone no farther than the Rice City National Bank. When it was discovered that he had substantial accounts there, everyone concerned would have been too embarrassed and apologetic to inquire further.

But as a murder suspect, the police would probe deeply into his background. It was almost certain that they would send a routine inquiry about him to the St. Louis police, inasmuch as the certified check he had deposited was on a St. Louis bank. And when the reply came labeling him as a notorious bunco artist, they'd have all the motive they needed.

Perhaps they wouldn't be able to figure out exactly what his game had been. But his peculiar actions would leave no doubt in their minds that he'd been in the process of working some kind of con game. And then assumption would be that he had killed Quincy because the man found him out.

To cinch the case against him there were Quincy's last words over the phone: "Hold it a sec, Joe. The door's opening." Even Horton had thought he meant the washroom door. Gannon certainly must have gotten the same impression.

The final thing which decided Horton that he had no chance at all was his realization that the police would probably welcome him as a patsy. With the murder following so closely upon publication of the anonymous threat Quincy had received, the Tony Manzetti mob would be automatically suspect in the public's mind, even if the racketeer had nothing to do with the killing. There was little doubt in Horton's mind that Manzetti had considerable control over the police department. If the police could take him off the hook by pinning the murder on Horton, they probably wouldn't hesitate to do it, even if they thought he might be innocent.

Rapidly he crossed to the phone and wiped it clear of prints with his handkerchief. Then he wiped off every other surface he thought he might have touched, both in the office and the washroom.

He was halfway out the door when he remembered his car registration. Turning, he scooped it from the desk and shoved it into his wallet.

As he drove off the lot, a siren sounded only a block away.

He made straight for the Hotel Lawford. He realized he had to check out at once, for his hotel and room number were on the back of the check he had given Trusting Joe Gannon. It would probably take the police a little time to discover this, for it was unlikely they would interview Gannon until they completed their preliminary investigation at the scene of the crime. But it was a certainty that they would get to the hotel eventually.

Even though he judged he had plenty of time to clear out of his room, he wouldn't have run the risk if it hadn't been essential. He had only twelve dollars in his wallet. One of his bags contained two hundred dollars in bills and five hundred in traveler's checks.

He was going to need all the cash he could get his hands on to take into hiding with him.

Parking across from the hotel, he crossed the street just as the red-haired desk clerk crossed from the diagonal corner. They met at the curb.

"Oh, hello, Mr. Horton," she said with a smile.

He smiled back mechanically. With an effort he slowed his stride to hers as they walked toward the hotel entrance together.

"Been on your lunch hour?" he asked.

She nodded, then grinned. "I never lunch at the hotel. Too expensive for the hired help."

He let her precede him through the revolving door and pushed through after her. He gave a quick glance about the lobby, and was reassured to see no police in evidence. Though he hadn't expected any this soon, he relaxed a little.

The girl had halted to wait for him. Stopping before her, he said, 'Would you do me a favor?"

"Why, of course," she said.

"I'm checking out. Will you tote up my bill so I can catch it on the fly? I'm in rather a hurry."

"You're leaving?" she asked in obvious disappointment.

"Not out of town," he said. She smiled, relieved. "You know, I tried to phone you last evening to invite you to dinner. But you'd just gone off duty."

"Oh, I'm sorry," she said in a tone indicating she meant it.

"Could I try again sometime? After I get settled."

"I'd love it," she said.

"I'll give you a ring. But you know, I don't know your name."

"Helen," she told him. "Helen Quincy."

He barely managed to suppress the startled expression he felt forming on his face. He asked casually, "Not related to that Quincy whose picture was in this morning's paper, are you?"

"Why, yes. I'm his step-daughter."

This time he was unable to keep his surprise from showing. "Step-daughter? You mean that blonde—Mr. Quincy's wife is your mother?"

Her eyes suddenly turned cool. "You know Velda?"

"Just barely. But certainly she's not old enough—"

"My mother is dead," she interrupted. "My father died when I was an infant, and mother married Quincy when I was five. He legally adopted me. Velda is his second wife." The cold manner in which she pronounced the name suggested that Quincy's second wife wasn't one of her favorite subjects.

Suddenly Horton realized that he was standing there chatting with the girl as though he had all the time in the world. The curse of overactive glands, he thought. With the police on his trail for murder, he had to take time out to line up a future conquest.

Abruptly he said, "I'd better get packed. You'll have my bill ready?"

"I'll add it up right away, Mr. Horton."

He was turning away, but he paused long enough to grin over his shoulder. "Make it Jim," he suggested.

She colored slightly. "All right, Jim," she said softly.

On the way up in the elevator he wondered about Helen Quincy. As the legally-adopted daughter of one of the town's most prominent citizens, it seemed strange that she worked as a hotel desk clerk. And her remark about the hotel's food being too expensive for her suggested that she had to be careful of her money.

Probably there was some kind of family estrangement, he decided. Possibly the blonde Velda was the cause of it. It wouldn't be unnatural for the girl to resent her stepfather taking as his second wife a glamorous woman not much older than herself.

In his room he transferred his money and his traveler's checks from his suitcase to his pockets. Then he packed quickly but without haste, feeling reasonably secure that the police would not get to the hotel for some time yet.

He had snapped the second of his two bags closed when the phone rang.

The sudden sound caused him to start nervously. He stared at the phone, making no move toward it, wondering what the ring meant. Possibly it was Belle or the colonel. No one else would be calling him.

Unless it was the police.

Then he relaxed as he realized the police would hardly phone. They'd simply knock on the door. He crossed to the phone and lifted it.

"Yes?" he said cautiously.

"Jim?" a low feminine voice said.

"Yes."

"Helen Quincy. I don't know what this is about, but I thought I'd better warn you. Two policemen are on their way up in the elevator."

Horton said, "Thanks, doll," and slammed down the receiver.

So much for his estimate of the time it would take the police to learn his local address, he thought, as he jerked open the room door and heaved his bags into the hall. In one continuous movement, he slammed the door shut behind him and scooped up the two bags again.

The elevators were only yards away, and he took a quick glance at the indicators. One showed a car already at third, and rising.

He headed for a turn in the corridor in the opposite direction at a dead run. Just as he rounded it, he heard the elevator door open. Setting down his bags, he leaned against the wall and listened.

Two pairs of footsteps approached, then stopped. A deep voice said, "This is it. Four fourteen." There was a loud knock.

CHAPTER VII

Halfway down the hall there was a fire exit. Horton stooped for his bags, then decided they were too encumbering for flight. Glancing along the hall at the various doors, he spotted one with no room number on it. Trying it, he found it open. It was a broom closet. He set his bags inside and pulled the door closed again.

Another, harder knock came from around the corner. The same deep voice he had heard before called, "Police officers, mister. Open up."

Quietly Horton walked to the fire exit and pushed open the door. It gave onto a windowless fire well. He went down the stairs quickly, but without running. The last half-flight was an open stairway leading into the lobby at a point right next to the side entrance. He slowed his descent of this to a normal walk.

Glancing toward the desk, he saw Helen Quincy staring at him from wide eyes. He lifted one hand in a casual salute, turned, and strolled from the side entrance.

Outside he turned right and walked toward the front of the hotel. At the corner he paused and looked across the street to where his car was parked.

Apparently the police had located and staked out his car before they entered the hotel after him. A uniformed officer stood on the sidewalk next to it.

Horton turned and retraced his steps to the street behind the hotel.

As he passed the side entrance, he wondered what Helen Quincy was thinking. He was thankful now that he had taken the time to talk to her in the lobby. He hoped he had charmed her enough to keep her silent about his leaving the hotel. Even though she had warned him that the police were on their way to his room, it seemed a lot to expect that she would cover his flight. She must have recognized it as flight. And there was the matter of his unpaid bill. He could only hope that the impression he had made on her was strong enough to counterbalance her loyalty to the hotel.

Momentarily he expected police to start pouring from the side entrance of the hotel in pursuit. But he reached the next intersection without anything happening.

He ran into some luck then. A cab neared the intersection just as he reached it, and stopped at his hail.

He had the taxi drop him at an intersection six blocks from the riverfront. Then he walked four more blocks in the direction of the river to Second Street.

In a used-clothing store on Second, he bought a cheap cloth cap to cover his tell-tale crew cut. He also bought a clean but worn leather jacket. At the next corner he bought a newspaper.

A half-block farther along, he entered a tavern crowded with workingmen. No one paid any attention as he walked to the men's room. Inside he changed his suit coat for the jacket and wrapped the coat in newspaper.

Studying his reflection in a mirror over the sink, he decided the cap and jacket made an adequate temporary disguise. In his present garb, except that his trousers were too well-pressed, his shoes too well-shined and he wore a necktie, he would be indistinguishable from hundreds of other men who lived in this neighborhood.

He rectified the first defect by removing his trousers and wadding and twisting them together. When he put them back on, they were satisfactorily wrinkled. A coating of liquid soap deadened the sheen of his shoes. Then he took off his tie, put it in his pocket and left his shirt collar open.

Leaving the tavern, he walked another block in the direction of the river to First Street. Turning left, back the way he had come, he wandered along First until he came to a seedy hotel exotically named the Palais Royal. It advertised rooms at a dollar and up.

The elderly man on duty behind the desk exhibited no interest in him when he registered as James Malone. Horton engaged a medium-priced room at a dollar seventy-five cents a day. At this price, rooms included a washbowl with both hot and cold running water. He would have preferred one of the two-fifty rooms, which had private baths, but he didn't want to invite undue attention.

He paid for two days in advance.

His room number was 212, on the second floor. The elderly desk clerk let him find it for himself. The Palais Royal didn't provide bell-boy service.

Horton surveyed his new home without enthusiasm. It was neither well-furnished nor very clean. A spotted green shade hung in the single curtainless window. Illumination was furnished by a naked light bulb hanging from the ceiling. The washbowl in the corner had a ring of dirt in it. The only furniture was a brass double bed, a dresser, and a wooden, straight-backed chair. A series of hooks along one wall served in lieu of a closet.

Horton drew back the bed covers and discovered with relief that at least the sheets were fresh. He also noted with some surprise that a phone stood on his dresser.

He secreted his newspaper-wrapped coat in the bottom dresser drawer. Then he lifted the phone.

After a short wait the voice of the elderly desk clerk said, "Yeah?"

Horton gave him the number of the Hotel Lawford. When the Lawford switchboard answered, he asked for room 727.

A moment later Belle Jarvis's voice said, "Hello."

"Hi, honey," Horton said.

"Jim!" she said in a pleased tone. "Where are you? In your room?"

"In a jam," he said.

Immediately she was concerned. "Something go wrong?"

"Everything. Want to do me a favor?"

"Of course, Jim. Just name it."

"Just a minute," he said. He paused for a second, then said, "Operator!"

When there was no reply, he said, "Just checking to make sure nobody was listening in. Right around the corner from my room you'll find a broom closet. My two bags are in it. Take them to your room and pack all my underwear, socks, shirts and shaving stuff in the smaller one. Leave everything else in the big one. And bring the smaller bag to me."

"Where are you?"

"Room 212 of the Palais Royal Hotel on First Street. Just walk in and up the stairs. I don't think anyone will stop you, but if they do, you're looking for James Malone. Incidentally, you'd better dress plainly. They're not used to class here. Got any old clothes?"

"Hmm," she said. "Some plain ones, I think. I'll manage. Expect me in half an hour."

"Make it forty-five minutes," he told her. "I haven't had time for lunch yet. I'm going out for some now."

It was typical of Belle that she hadn't asked what his trouble was before offering to help.

He found a coffee shop a block from the Palais Royal. It was the sort of place where he could sit at the counter wearing his cap without being conspicuous. He lunched on a greasy hamburger and a cup of bitter coffee.

Back in his room he had barely hung his cap and jacket on a pair of the wall hooks when Belle rapped on the door. She came in quickly when he opened it. He took the bag from her hand, dropped it on the floor next to the dresser and looked her over. She wore a plain gray sweater with a matching skirt which would have been appropriate on either a cafe-society habitué or a working girl. Plain black pumps without stockings would have inclined the casual observer to guess her the latter.

Horton nodded approvingly.

She offered her lips for a kiss, and he brushed them lightly with his own. Then she looked around the room.

"Well, well," she said. "So this is how the other half lives. Sure you can afford it?"

"It's a strain," he said. "Considering that the bulk of my wealth is on deposit at the Rice City National Bank. And if I go near the place, lurking cops will probably make with the handcuffs."

"It's that bad?" she asked with concern. "What happened? Your mark get wise to you?"

"Worse than that. He got murdered."

Her eyes widened.

"Not by me," he hastened to add. "I was just an innocent bystander. But the cops think it was me."

She said, "If you'll open your bag, you'll find I included a bottle of liquor. I think I need a drink before I hear about this."

He snapped open the bag, drew out a fifth of bonded bourbon and flashed Belle a look of admiration. "You always were a thoughtful kitten," he said. "Afraid there's no ice, but we do have water."

There were two jelly glasses on the dresser. Horton washed them in hot water, poured a couple of ounces of whisky into each and added cold water. When he handed Belle hers, she carried it over to the bed and sat down.

Leaning against the dresser, Horton raised his glass. "Cheers," he said.

Belle tossed off half of her drink and shuddered. Horton barely sipped his, set it on the dresser and produced a package of cigarettes. He offered Belle one, put another in his mouth and held flame to both. Lifting an ash tray from the dresser, he set it on the bed next to Belle.

Belle inhaled deeply and blew thin streams of smoke from her nostrils. "Now, tell me what happened," she said.

CHAPTER VIII

Horton took it from the beginning, outlining his actions from the moment he had hit town until the moment of the murder. When he finished, Belle's expression was a mixture of concern for his plight and admiration for the bunco game he had worked out.

"What a fool-proof gimmick," she said with enthusiasm. "Jim, there's no doubt about it. You're a genius." Then she gave him a puzzled frown. "But why all the extra trimmings?"

"What extra trimmings?"

"Well, the plot was to get yourself arrested for passing a hot check, wasn't it? And then, after the banks opened Monday and your check proved good, to sue everybody in sight for false arrest, defamation of character and personal indignity."

"Yeah," he said regretfully. "I didn't see how it could miss."

"It couldn't under ordinary circumstances," she assured him. "Why, it's almost legal!"

"Entirely legal," he corrected. "I couldn't have been held for anything, even if it blew up." He added ruefully, "Except on a bum rap like this."

"Still, why did you need all the extra trimmings? I mean like the appointment with Acme Realty to view beach homes, arranging with the bank for a mortgage and so on? Why not just buy your car in one lot, drive to another and offer to sell it cheap? You'd get arrested just as fast."

Horton shook his head reprovingly. "You really don't have a con-woman's mind, Belle. Sure, I'd get arrested just as fast. And get my case kicked out of court even faster."

"Why?" she asked. "It would still be false arrest."

"Uh-huh. Except that it would stick out a mile as a con game. The police couldn't wait to get off a wire to St. Louis asking for a record search. And when they got back the news that I've conned half the people in the Midwest out of their savings, you think anybody would pay off? Even a green lawyer could convince a jury that I deliberately got myself arrested for the sole purpose of bringing suit."

After thinking this over, Belle said doubtfully, "I suppose."

"My way, they'd never look farther than Rice City. Acme Realty Company could give evidence that I had a *bona fide* intention of buying a summer home here. Hanford Maytum at the bank could testify that I inquired about a mortgage. And, more important, that I'm a nut on sport cars, particularly Jaguars. The salesman at Gannon's would have to admit I wanted to buy a Jaguar before he talked me into a Mercury by assuring me I wouldn't find a used Jaguar in town. A jury might question my business sense in taking a thousand-dollar loss on a car I'd owned less than a half hour, but they'd pass it off as the eccentricity of a guy who was overboard on Jaguars. And look how much greater my loss is the way I worked it than the way you suggest."

Belle said, "I don't follow you."

"Naturally I'm not going to live in a town which treats me so shabbily. I drop all plans to buy a summer home. Not only have I suffered great indignity, I've been forced to change major living plans. After I slapped suits for a hundred thousand each against Trusting Joe Gannon, Honest John Quincy and the city, all three should have been willing to settle out of court for twenty-five thousand apiece."

This time Belle's face expressed complete understanding. "I guess I do lack a con-woman's mind. You *are* a genius."

"Some genius," Horton said bitterly. "It takes an idiot to get himself in a jam like this." Viciously he ground out his cigarette.

Belle had been so engrossed in Horton's description of his bunco game, momentarily she had forgotten his plight. Now her expression grew worried again.

"What are you going to do, Jim? Run?"

He shook his head. "The police have never made a beef stick against me yet. Anywhere. I'm not about to take a fall now for something I didn't do."

"You're going to fight it?"

"Not in court, if that's what you mean. In this town I wouldn't stand a chance if I turned myself in. My only hope is to find the real killer."

Belle considered this dubiously. "Is there any way I can help?" she asked.

"You might tell me what you know about Quincy. Didn't you mention that you and the colonel picked him for your first mark?"

"Until we found out who he was and veered off. I really don't know a thing about him that I haven't already told you."

"You must know something," he insisted. "I've seen you operate. Men pour their life stories in your ear."

"We dropped him too quickly," Belle said. "I simply met him at the Lawford's bar and felt him out enough to find out he was loaded with money. He gave me the usual line about his wife not understanding him, but aside from that I didn't delve into his personal life. He didn't even mention that he was chairman of the Civic Crime Committee. The colonel found that out the next day, when he began checking up on the man. We decided conning someone with his connections was too dangerous, and started looking for another mark. I never saw Quincy after that first casual meeting in the bar."

"Hmm," Horton said. "I'd hoped you could give me some kind of lead. Guess I'll have to scrounge around somewhere else."

Belle stubbed out her cigarette and took a thoughtful sip of her drink. "Won't your description be in the newspapers? You'll be recognized the moment you step outdoors. You're not exactly ordinary-looking."

Instead of answering, Horton moved to the wall hooks, shrugged into his leather jacket, and pulled on his cap with the peak low over his eyes. He thrust his hands in his pockets and slouched across the room.

Belle regarded him with her mouth open. For the first time she noted the wrinkled trousers and lusterless shoes. Suddenly, despite her worry for him, she laughed.

"Better modify the walk," she advised. "You'll get picked up for vagrancy."

He hung up the jacket and cap again. "I think I'll be safe enough," he said. "Unless I run into somebody I know. And there aren't more than a half dozen people in town aside from you and the colonel who know me by sight."

"Colonel Bob and I will help all we can, of course," Belle said. "Need any money?"

Horton shook his head. "I have about two hundred in cash. Plus five hundred in traveler's checks." He smiled ruefully. "Lot of good those will do, though. By the time the banks open Monday, my name will be splashed all over the papers. I wouldn't dare try cashing one."

"Maybe the colonel can do some leg work," she suggested. "Poke around at Police Headquarters to find out what they know, for instance."

Horton raised his eyebrows. "Aren't you about set to skin your mark? Won't you be leaving town rather suddenly?"

"That can wait," she said. "He's set up to take the bait now, as a matter of fact. But we can stall until this is settled. The colonel can always get a tip from one of his inside-Wall-Street contacts advising delay."

"Uh-uh," Horton said. "I'm not going to upset your plans."

Belle rose from the bed, set her glass on the dresser and put her hands on his shoulders.

Looking up at him, she said, "Do you think either the colonel or I would run out on you in a spot like this? Even if it meant missing out with our mark altogether?"

"It's too risky, Belle. If things went wrong, both of you could be charged as accessories for helping me. I won't let you do it."

She gave him an exasperated smile. "You don't understand, do you, you big lug?"

"Understand what?"

"That I love you."

Horton stared down at her. It wasn't a new experience for him to be told he was loved by a woman. Dozens had said it, despite his careful avoidance of the subject himself. Usually he was adroit at changing the subject without either offending the lady or letting her realize he was deliberately skirting entanglement.

This time he was caught completely off-center. He had a genuine regard for Belle, genuine enough not to want to see her hurt in any way. But the thought of love had never entered his head. He had assumed her amatory interest in him was as casual as his in her. Suddenly, for the first time in his life, he felt like a heel.

Seeing the look on his face, she dropped her hands from his shoulders. Her expression became rueful.

"I didn't expect reciprocation," she said. "There's too much wolf in you to settle for one woman. But you don't have to look so woebegone."

"Who's looking woebegone?" he protested.

"You. You look as guilty as a teen-ager caught behind the garage with the little girl from next door. If it's any salve to your conscience, last night had nothing to do with it."

"Huh?" he said a little stupidly.

"I've been overboard about you from the day the colonel introduced us. Four years ago." She laughed shortly. "I used to tell myself it was just a case of puppy love that I'd get over. I was only twenty-three then, you know. But it wasn't. Last night didn't change anything. It just confirmed what I knew all along. That you're wonderful."

He looked at her helplessly for a moment, then turned toward the dresser, lifted his glass and tossed off the rest of his unfinished drink. Immediately he poured two more. He added water from the washbowl tap and carried the glasses back to the dresser. Silently he handed her one.

She raised her glass with a smile on her lips. "To unrequited love."

Horton said, "That's hardly fair."

"What woman is fair?" she inquired. "Come on. Bottoms up."

He followed her advice. He needed the drink. When he set down his empty glass, he saw that she had tossed off all of hers too. She set her glass next to his on the dresser.

"Let's get something straight," she said.

"What?"

"I wouldn't have mentioned how I felt if you hadn't turned down my offer. I just wanted you to know I *have* to help. I don't want you treating me with kid gloves, afraid that I'll twist something you say into a declaration of love. When this is over, you'll go your way and I'll go mine. Meantime, all I expect from you is to be treated like a woman."

He looked at her for a long time, finally grinned. "How is that?"

"You've had enough experience," she said. "You ought to know."

He grinned at her again, then took her by the shoulders and drew her into his arms.

CHAPTER IX

Belle stayed until six P.M. Before she left, they settled the matter of future contacts.

Horton insisted that neither she nor Colonel Bob visit the Palais Royal again, because of the danger of them being tabbed as accessories in case the police suddenly walked in. Future contacts would be in public places so that, if Horton was taken by the police during a conference with one or the other of them, they could claim it was a casual encounter and they had never seen him before.

Belle said she would start the colonel digging for information right away, and would phone him the next morning.

Shortly after Belle left, Horton donned his cap and jacket and went out to find some dinner. He located a hamburger stand on Third Street where the food was a little more edible than at the place he had lunched, but where he still wouldn't be conspicuous by wearing his cap at the counter. He bought an evening paper from a newsboy just outside the hamburger stand, and read it while waiting to be served.

The murder of Honest John Quincy was splashed all over the front page. As Horton had expected, he got full credit for it.

The account read:

> "Honest" John Quincy, local car dealer and chairman of the Civic Crime Committee, died of a gunshot wound about noon today, only sixteen hours after receiving a threat against his life. An anonymous note consisting of words cut from a newspaper and pasted on a piece of paper had been found by Quincy in his residence mailbox at 223 River Road at eight o'clock Friday evening. The note read: "Call off your dogs, snooper, or you're done. This is your last warning. Next you get a bullet."
>
> Police, however, do not believe the killing was an outcome of the threat. They base their opinion on their alleged knowledge of who the killer is.
>
> The shooting took place in the office of the used-car lot operated by Quincy in downtown Rice City. The deceased was speaking on the phone to Joseph Cannon, the operator of another used-car lot, when

he was murdered. Gannon, who heard the shot fired over the phone, reported to police the identity of the alleged killer.

According to Lieutenant Thomas Gray, head of the Homicide Squad, Quincy was killed by a man attempting to pass a bad check. Quincy was phoning Gannon to ask him to call the police when he was shot. It is believed that the killer overheard the call and shot Quincy to avoid arrest.

The lieutenant identified the alleged killer as a man going under the name of James Horton and, until shortly after the murder, residing at the Hotel Lawford. The suspect eluded arrest by a narrow margin when police arrived at his hotel room shortly after he absconded without paying his bill. An all-points bulletin is out for his arrest.

The suspect is described as six-feet-two to six-feet-three, a hundred and ninety to two hundred pounds, with a muscular build. He is about thirty years old, has sandy hair worn in a crew cut. When last seen, he wore a tan gabardine suit. Anyone seeing a man of this description is asked to phone the police immediately.

The suspect's home address was listed at the Lawford as St. Louis. Lieutenant Grady said that a wire had already been sent to St. Louis requesting a record check. However, the Homicide chief is of the opinion that James Horton is probably an alias, and said he does not expect much result from the St. Loius wire.

Grady said there was no question in his mind that the murder had no connection with the anonymous threat Quincy received yesterday, which he attributes to some crank.

Asked his opinion of Quincy's charge, as reported in this morning's edition, that the threat had been sent by the Tony Manzetti machine, Lieutenant Grady rejected the idea.

"As far as I know, Mr. Manzetti is just a politician," he said. "If he's got a machine of some kind, I never heard of it."

The remainder of the article was a rehash of that morning's item about the anonymous threat. It ended with the usual statement that the police were working on several leads and expected to make an arrest in the near future.

Horton's dinner came, and he folded up the paper.

Any remote hope he had that the police might at least consider the possibility that it had been a gangland kill now faded completely. Obviously they were content with him as the sole suspect. And Lieutenant Grady's performance left little doubt that he was an obedient tool of the Manzetti machine, and would do nothing which might tend to incriminate the political and racket boss.

* * * *

The next morning, Sunday, Horton stayed in his room awaiting Belle's promised phone call. It didn't come until nearly noon.

When she finally phoned, she said, "Sorry to be so late, but I just this minute heard from the colonel."

"He get anything?" Horton asked.

"I don't know. He did some poking around last night. Mainly just making contacts, I think. Then this morning he was off to Police Headquarters, and he just phoned that he's lunching with a reporter. He wants you to meet him at two this afternoon."

"Where?"

"A tavern near the Rafferty House. The Hurricane Bar at 611 Concord. He says it's a quiet neighborhood place with a mixed clientele, where neither a Beau Brummell nor a bum would attract attention."

"He's the Beau Brummell, I suppose," Horton said.

Belle chuckled. "Well, I told him about your new outfit. He's looking forward to seeing it. I hope you haven't shaved today. He'll be disappointed."

"I haven't," Horton assured her. "I wouldn't spoil his kick for the world."

After Belle hung up, Horton went out and had some lunch. Then he decided to walk to the Hurricane Bar. It was four miles, but he had nothing else to do. He took it slowly and arrived a few minutes past two.

The place was an ordinary neighborhood tavern, clean but unpretentious. Horton peered through the plate-glass window and saw the colonel at the bar in conversation with a thin, gray-haired man wearing rimless glasses. The man was as well-dressed as the colonel. The only other customer was a man in a coverall at the far end of the bar.

A dour-looking bartender seemed to be listening intently to the conversation between the colonel and the thin man.

Horton went in and took a seat at the near end of the bar. Colonel Bob looked at him with no sign of recognition. When the bartender came forward, Horton ordered a beer.

The colonel had one eyebrow raised and was staring at the thin, gray-haired man through his invisible monocle. His ragged mustache bristled belligerently. He was saying, "I don't care if you are a teacher of English, sir. I myself am a retired army officer. They don't exactly turn dunces out of West Point, you know."

"I wasn't inferring you lack education," the thin man protested. "I merely said you are quite wrong if you think any word beginning with Q doesn't require a U as its second letter. A U *always* follows Q."

The colonel turned to the dour bartender. "Do you have a dictionary, my good fellow?"

There were three books in plain sight stacked together on the back-bar: an almanac, a street guide and Webster's Collegiate Dictionary. The colonel couldn't have helped seeing them, and Horton suspected the sight of the dictionary had inspired whatever small con game he was in the process of working.

Horton sighed to himself. Colonel Bob couldn't resist taking a mark when the oportunity offered, even if the potential take amounted to as little as a dime. Horton knew there was no point in interrupting the game. The colonel would give his attention to him only when the matter at hand was completed.

The bartender lifted the dictionary from the backbar and placed it in front of the colonel. Taking out his wallet, Colonel Bob slapped a fifty-dollar bill on the bar.

He said, "I will wager this fifty or any part of it that this dictionary defines at least one word beginning with Q whose second letter is not U."

The English teacher looked at him quizzically. "You'd lose your money."

"A calculated risk I'm prepared to take," the colonel retorted. "Do you accept, sir?"

The thin man looked at him for a moment more. "You said 'defines' the word. It isn't some kind of abbreviation used in footnotes? It's an actual word which Webster defines?"

"An actual word," the colonel assured him.

The English teacher took out his wallet. He laid a twenty, a ten and two fives on the bar. He said to the bartender, "George, lend me ten dollars."

CHAPTER X

The bartender had pulled the book toward him and had opened it to the Q's. He was running his finger down the columns of each page, flipping the pages as he finished his examination of each.

He said, "Just a minute, Professor," and went on flipping pages.

When he finished, he went back to the first page and checked it again. It didn't take him long, as there were only seven pages in the Q section. Then he closed the book, took a ten from the cash register and slapped it on top of the English teacher's forty dollars.

"Want to cover some more?" he asked the colonel.

Colonel Bob frowned at him. "You've already checked the book, sir."

"Well, you're so doggoned sure of yourself."

"Very well," the colonel said agreeably. "Possibly I'm in error, and the word I have in mind appears only in Webster's unabridged. But I've already committed my troops, so I'll back them with every gun."

He took another fifty from his wallet and laid it on the bar.

The bartender said, "It has to be in this here book. It don't count if it's in some other dictionary."

"Agreed," the colonel submitted.

"And it has to be a defined word, like the professor said."

"Agreed."

The bartender rang up "no sale" again, took another fifty dollars from the register and slapped it on the bar.

"Okay, mister. You just show us that word."

The man wearing the coverall had come forward from the far end of the bar in order to better view the betting activity. The colonel said to him, "You wish to risk a wager too, sir?"

The man considered, then shook his head. "I'll just watch."

Colonel Bob glanced down at Horton. Horton grinned and gave him a headshake.

The colonel turned back to the bartender. "Turn to the Gazetteer in the back of the book, please."

"Huh?" the bartender said.

"I didn't say *where* in the dictionary the word would be found," Colonel Bob said. "I merely stipulated that it would be defined in that book. It's in the Gazetteer section. The word is Q-I-S-H-M, pronounced 'Kishum.' It's an island in the Strait of Hormuz in South Persia."

The English teacher reached for the book before the bartender could get his hands on it. He opened it and riffled pages until he reached the 'Q' section of the Pronouncing Gazetteer. He stared at the page with his jaw hanging in surprise.

Then he looked up as a thought struck him. "Wait a minute. This can't be an English word. It must be Persian."

"Who stipulated it had to be English?" the colonel asked, picking up the money. "Certainly I didn't. I merely said Webster defined it. Thank you, gentlemen, for a very pleasant conversation."

And he sauntered out of the tavern.

Horton finished his beer and followed. The English teacher and the bartender were still staring at the door with their mouths open. The man in the coverall was grinning.

Colonel Bob was a half-block away, strolling down Concord Avenue toward the next intersection. Horton shambled along after him with his hands in his pockets.

At the corner the colonel took a seat on a bus-stop bench, drew the folded sport section of the Sunday newspaper from his pocket, and opened it. A few moments later Horton sank down onto the bench next to him.

Without looking at him, the colonel said, "Sorry, my good man. Don't believe in giving handouts. Only encourages laziness. Why can't you work for a living, like the rest of us?"

"Very funny," Horton said. "Find anything?"

"A good deal more than appeared in the newspapers," the colonel said with a touch of self-importance. He turned his head and hiked an eyebrow to fix Horton with his invisible monocle. "Remarkable how co-operative people are with professional writers."

"Oh? You're a professional writer now?"

"True crime story free-lancer. With an assignment to cover yesterday's murder."

He drew a telegram from his pocket and handed it to Horton. The sender's address was New York City, and it was addressed to Major Herbert Walsh in care of the Rafferty House. It read:

WIRE SERVICES REPORT MURDER RICE CITY CIVIC CRIME COMMITTEE CHAIRMAN. SINCE YOU'RE ON SCENE, CAN YOU COVER FOR FOUR THOUSAND WORD STORY. WILL

PAY YOUR USUAL RATE OF TEN CENTS PER WORD PLUS EX-
PENSES. JUNE 30 DEADLINE. CONFIRM BY RETURN WIRE.
AL GATES
EDITOR FACT CRIME MAGAZINE

Handing back the wire, Horton asked, "Who sent it?"

"Friend of mine in New York. I phoned him long-distance at seven last night, and had the wire an hour later. Peculiar how people will accept a telegram as authentic credentials. Minute I showed it, the police threw open their files. I'm getting the real red-carpet treatment. They all hope I'll mention them in the article, you see."

"Human nature," Horton siad. "What've you learned?"

"Well, for one thing, they all think you did it. Not just the police. Even the reporters I've talked to who aren't inclined to favor the Manzetti mob. The papers would love to stick Manzetti with it, but the evidence against you is too strong."

"Yeah," Horton said sourly. "I read the news account."

"I did get one encouraging bit from a reporter I lunched with today. To a man the local press is convinced that the Manzetti mob was behind that threat. They can't say it in print, of course, because of the criminal libel laws. They went as far as they could by quoting Quincy. This reporter I lunched with says it's quite in keeping with Tony Manzetti's normal behavior. Describes him as a throwback to the 1920's. An arrogant, strutting gangster who thinks he can get away with anything so long as he has his hired guns behind him. They think he probably would have had Quincy gunned eventually, if you hadn't saved him the trouble."

"Hmm. What did you get from the police?"

"The murder bullet was from a forty-five-caliber pistol. Ballistics couldn't match it with anything on file. The weapon hasn't been found. Probably at the bottom of the river by now. Oh, yes. A nice set of your fingerprints was found on the inside of the washroom door."

Horton looked startled. "When I pressed my ear to the door," he said ruefully. "I forgot that when I was wiping off surfaces. How'd they match them?"

"Your record came in from St. Louis this morning. Describes you as a notorious con man whom half the police departments in the Midwest have been trying to nail for years. How did you ever manage seventeen arrests without a conviction?"

"Genius," Horton said bitterly. "I only take falls for crimes I don't commit."

"Things don't look good," the colonel said. "According to your version of what happened, it seems likely the killer was a Manzetti gun. But how would you ever prove it?"

"Where's this Manzetti hang out?"

"His headquarters is the Sixth Ward Athletic Club, down near the river on Gibbons Street between Second and Third. The club is party headquarters for the Sixth Ward. Manzetti's committeeman for that ward, you know."

"No, I didn't. Think you could find out from your reporter friend who the likely gunman would have been, if it was a Manzetti kill?"

Colonel Bob looked dubious. "I can try. But you're not planning a frontal attack on a force as powerful as Manzetti, are you? You'll get yourself killed."

"I'll get myself killed by the state if I don't," Horton said. "What's there to lose?"

At that moment a uniformed policeman appeared on the corner opposite them. He strolled across the street, swinging his club. The colonel buried his nose in his paper and Horton slouched down in his seat.

The officer gave them a casual glance as he passed, then moved on.

The colonel gave Horton a quizzical sideglance. "Well, you passed that inspection."

"Yeah," Horton said, expelling a breath of relief. "But I aged a year. I *have* to clean this up, Colonel. I'm not going to spend the rest of my life hiding out in flophouses and dressing like a bum."

"Know how you feel," the colonel said sympathetically. "I've had the same queasy feeling myself when a minion of the law glanced at me. And I've never been wanted for anything that would bring more than a couple of years. Must make clammy sweat spring to the brow, knowing the bluecoats want to start you walking that long, last mile."

Horton threw him a cold look. "Keep reminding me. I like to think about death row." He stood up. "When can you see your reporter friend again?"

"I'll invite him over to the hotel for dinner tonight. Phone you at your room later if I learn anything."

"Fine," Horton said. "And thanks for everything. I know all this is interfering with your own plans."

The colonel raised an eyebrow. "Matter of duty, old man. If we didn't stick together in our lonely profession, where would we be? Don't even mention it."

Horton gave him a grin of good-by and shambled off down the street with his hands in his pockets.

CHAPTER XI

At nine that evening, the colonel phoned. He didn't preface what he had to say with either a greeting or an announcement of his name. If Horton hadn't recognized his voice, he wouldn't have known who was calling.

All the colonel said was, "Phone me at Circle 3320 from a booth." Then he hung up.

Donning his cap and jacket, Horton walked a block to an all-night drugstore, shut himself into a phone booth and dialed the number. It was answered in the middle of the first ring.

"This is better," the colonel's voice said. "Pay phone to pay phone. Don't like talking through a switchboard."

"Learn anything?" Horton asked.

"Manzetti has a number of hatchet men. But his top one is a character known as Joey the Cut. Legal name Joseph Ault. My friend thinks Manzetti would use him for anything important."

"Joey the Cut, eh?"

"Yes. Childlike, the names some of these underworld people assume, isn't it? In this case the man has a livid scar on his left cheek, but that isn't the reason for his name. He had the name before he got the cut."

"Oh?"

"The name comes from his onetime job of collecting Manzetti's share of the take from illegal gambling dives. He came after the cut, you see."

"Uh-huh. Where's he hang out?"

"Where all of them do. At the Sixth Ward Athletic Club. It's sort of the hub of social life in that area. But it won't do you much good to find him."

"Why not?"

"He doesn't even talk to his friends, let alone strangers. As a matter of fact, he's rumored to have no friends except Tony Manzetti."

"How do you get in the Sixth Ward Athletic Club?"

"You don't, if you have any sense. But I suppose you'll ignore my advice. You just walk in."

"Just like that?"

"There's a barroom on the first floor," the colonel explained, "theoretically reserved for members and guests, but anybody can get in. Nobody checks the door. Manzetti uses the place as a means of cementing the political vote. Has low bar prices, throws a lot of free feeds. Workingmen from the Sixth Ward flock there. He wanders around playing the congenial host. Calls everybody by their first names, inquires about their families, buys lots of drinks on the house. Comes polling time, customers return the favor by voting the way he suggests. He delivers an overwhelming majority for the party every election."

"He just controls that one ward?" Horton asked. "What makes him so powerful, then?"

"Biggest ward in the city. Contains eight percent of the total registered vote. Enough to swing local elections either way he wants. Gives him a say in the appointment of every important local office from the D.A. on down. Don't underestimate the man."

"I won't," Horton said. "Anything else?"

"Not about Manzetti. My reporter friend dropped another interesting little item, though."

"What?"

"Quincy was married to a woman twenty-five years his junior. Gorgeous blonde named Velda."

"I know. I've met her."

"Oh?" the colonel said with surprise. "Anyway, it's common gossip that at the gentlest push she'll fall in the hay with anyone. Recently there's been a rumor that Quincy was fed up to here. Had a private eye gathering divorce evidence."

"Yeah?"

"If he'd gotten a divorce on adultery, he wouldn't have had to pay alimony. Occurred to me that if Manzetti wasn't behind this, she might have taken advantage of all the publicity about the threat to get herself off the hook and let Manzetti take the rap."

Horton said dubiously, "With a forty-five? Women usually don't go for such heavy artillery."

"Maybe it was the only gun she had access to. And even discounting the divorce rumor, she certainly had a beautiful motive."

"What's that?"

"My reporter friend estimates Quincy's estate will run upwards of a million dollars."

After the colonel hung up, Horton mused over the new angle of Velda being a possible suspect. It was certainly worth looking into, he decided. But the first order of business was still Manzetti.

The Sixth Ward Athletic Club was less than two miles north of the Palais Royal. The Sunday-night closing hour for bars was midnight, so he had plenty of time. He decided to walk it.

He wasn't too afraid of recognition by anyone at the Athletic Club. In addition to his semi-shabby clothing, he now had a day's growth of sandy-colored beard. With his cap hiding his crew cut, he resembled his newspaper description very little. He looked as though he might be a truck driver or a factory laborer.

He reached the club just before ten. It was a rambling, three-story frame building, all dark at this time of night except for the corner containing the barroom.

Pushing open one side of a wide double door in the building's center, he found himself in a dimly-lighted hallway. To his left was a door labeled "Gymnasium." Ahead were stairs leading to the upper floors. To his right, noise spilled from the open door of the barroom.

He went through the door into an enormous room crowded with tables and flanked by a bar which must have been forty feet long. Three aproned, shirt-sleeved bartenders were on duty. There weren't more than three or four vacant places the whole length of the bar, and no vacant tables. Small-stakes games of poker, rummy and pinochle were under way at several of the tables. At others groups of men and women sat eating and drinking. Most of the women were dressed cheaply, and many of the men wore work clothes. There weren't a half-dozen neckties in the place.

The buzz of conversation, bursts of laughter and the clink of glasses created a subdued roar which enveloped the whole place.

Horton moved into one of the vacant places at the bar and ordered a beer. He could understand the club's popularity when the bartender set it before him. It was a fourteen-ounce stein, and the charge was a dime.

Numbers of people were wandering around the room, some table hopping, some standing behind card players watching the play, others merely carrying drinks to tables. Horton decided it wouldn't be conspicuous for him to make a circuit of the place. Carrying his beer, he wandered among the tables looking the men over. He spotted no one with a scar such as the colonel had described.

He had no trouble tabbing Tony Manzetti, however. The man swaggered around the room like a benevolent tyrant, slapping backs, roaring friendly insults and buying drinks. He was a short, wide, powerfully-built man with heavy features and a broad mouth which was perpetually split in a grin to expose large, beautifully-white teeth. His complexion was dark and his hair clung close to his scalp in thick, dark ringlets. He was in his shirtsleeves, but the gray trousers he wore suggested that the suit of which they were a part was in the two-hundred-dollar class. His shirt was white nylon and he wore a dark-red silk necktie with a diamond-studded, gold tie-clip. Horton judged he was about forty-five.

Horton was returning to the bar when he heard Manzetti roar, "Hey, Joey's here! Now watch the joint jump."

He turned to see Manzetti near the door with his hand on the shoulder of a new arrival. There was no doubt that it was Joey the Cut. A livid scar ran the length of the man's left cheek, from ear to chin.

Joey Ault was tall and bone lean, with eyes deepset in a pale, thin face. Apparently Manzetti's remark was in the nature of a joke, because everyone around him laughed dutifully.

Joey didn't join in the forced mirth. His expression remained humorless.

Manzetti gave his number-one hatchet man a friendly pat on the back and moved on to shout a comment to one of the groups of card players. Joey the Cut made his way to the bar.

Horton waited until the man picked a place, then moved to the bar next to him. Setting down his beer, he said, "Boy, it's really crowded tonight, isn't it?"

Joey gave him a bare glance. "It always is," he said. He ordered a shot and a beer from the bartender.

Horton waited until he had tossed off the shot, drunk half his beer and ordered another shot before he ventured another remark. Then he said, "It's a wonder any other bar in town gets any business, the way Tony gives this place away."

The dour hatchet man, after his brief reply to Horton's first comment, had looked straight ahead and paid him no further attention. Now he looked sidewise and studied Horton for a moment.

"It's his place," he said finally.

"Oh, I wasn't kicking," Horton said. "I like it. Hardly ever go anywhere else."

Joey looked forward again, tossed off his shot and finished his beer. Horton drained his beer also and signaled to one of the bartenders.

"Buy you a drink?" he asked Joey.

The man glanced at him again. "Why?"

Horton shrugged. "Why not? Tony's been buying me drinks for weeks. Ever since the first time I came in here. Thought I ought to buy somebody a drink for a change."

"Why don't you buy Tony one?"

Horton frowned at him. "What's eating you, mister? All I'm doing is trying to be friendly. You want a drink or don't you?"

Joey regarded him without expression. Finally he said, "Sure, I'll have one."

The bartender drew two beers and poured a shot for Joey. Horton paid for the drinks.

"Luck," Joey said, and took a sip of his beer.

Horton said, "Drink hearty," and sipped his.

With a curious mixture of apology and pride, Joey suddenly said, "Nobody buys me drinks, usually. You must be new around here."

"About a month," Horton said. "Why don't they buy you drinks?"

"Know who I am?"

"I heard Tony call you Joey."

"I'm Joey Ault."

"Oh, yeah," Horton said in a slightly different tone. He put a faint touch of awe in it. "I've heard of you."

"Then you know why nobody buys me drinks."

Horton looked at him. "Not me. Why?"

"They're afraid of me," Joey said matter-of-factly.

Horton cocked an eyebrow at him. "Why? I'm not."

Joey's face became very still. He stared at Horton unblinkingly. In a soft voice he said, "You're a brave man."

Horton looked puzzled, then let his expression clear. "Hey, you took me wrong. I mean, why should I be? I've got no beef with you. I get along with everybody. I'm not trying to be brave. Just friendly."

"Oh," Joey said, relaxing. He drank half his whisky and chased it with a gulp of beer.

Horton chuckled. "You think I was trying to choose you? Do I look that nuts?"

For the first time something approaching a smile appeared on the hatchet man's face. It wasn't quite a smile, but it was definitely a pleased look.

CHAPTER XII

Horton had struck exactly the right chord with Joey. He had flattered his reputation without exhibiting fear of the man. And he was being companionable. Except for the patronizing, back-slapping way he was treated by Tony Manzetti, no one ever offered Joey companionship. They were all too scared of him. He responded as a love-starved spinster would have responded to a wink and a wolf whistle.

The man actually became garrulous. He poured forth opinions, unfolded the history of his life, and told several dirty jokes. And he insisted on buying drinks. Horton had three beers he didn't want.

Joey meantime had three more boilermakers. Ordinarily drink only made him more morose, but tonight he expanded. His thin features became flushed and his face assumed a fixed grin. The bartender serving them watched him in amazement.

By eleven-thirty, Joey was in a state of alcoholic bliss. Laying a hand on Horton's shoulder, he said, "Heard Tony tell a good one the other day. This'll kill you."

Horton decided it was time to steer the conversation where he wanted it. "Tony's a card, all right," he said. "Lucky, too. Sure glad that killing yesterday turned out so good for him."

"Huh?" Joey said.

"That Quincy guy. Sure is lucky the cops know who did it. After that threat, the finger would have pointed straight at Tony."

Joey blinked owlishly. "Wanna know something?" he asked.

"What?"

"Ev'body thinks Tony sent that threat. Even some of 'a boys. He don't allus tell 'em everything's going on, see. But me, I know." He tapped his chest. "I'm 'a boss's righthand man. He don't keep nothing from me."

"No fooling?"

Joey wagged his head back and forth. "Not one l'il thing. And you know what?"

"What?"

"Tony din't send that note. The guy who killed Quincy did."

"You mean the hot-check artist?"

Joey laughed. "He wasn't no hot-check artist. Old Man Maytum from Rice City National phoned the cops when he seen the paper. Tole 'em the guy had fifteen gran' on deposit there. His checks was good."

"I'll be darned," Horton said.

Joey's voice sank confidentially. "Know what Tony thinks?"

"What?"

"This broad Quincy was married to set the whole thing up. Hired this guy to do the job. He hadda record in Missouri a mile long."

"A bad one, eh?" Horton said.

"A pro. Way Tony figures, the Quincy dame knows the firs' place the cops look when a guy gets bumped is at his wife. So she throws a curve. Has her hired gun drop off that note the night before the job. Then ev'body's supposed to think Tony ordered it." He looked a little aggrieved. "Like Tony would pull a deal that sloppy."

Horton didn't say anything. He was thinking that the colonel wasn't the only one who had cast a suspicious eye at the blonde Velda. He had the hopeful thought that perhaps the police were considering her, too. Then he felt depressed again as he realized this wouldn't take him off the hook if their thinking followed the same line as Tony Manzetti's. It would just revise their theory of his motive.

"Only the guy loused up," Joey went on. "He'd bought a car, see. Just a few minutes 'fore he hit Quincy's place. He hadda have an excuse to hang around. Tony figures maybe some other customer was there, and he hadda stall till they left. So he says he wants to sell the car. Then he goes off to the washroom. Quincy's s'picious, so he phones the place the guy bought the car. Tells the other car dealer all about it. The guy comes out of the washroom and shoots him while he's still talkin' onna phone. He don't know Quincy has tole the guy he's talking to who he is. So the whole deal backfires. You see—"

The amazed voice of Tony Manzetti interrupted. "Whataya' know!" he boomed. "The Sphinx is actually talking! A mile a minute, too. What's with you, Joey?"

Horton turned to find the racketeer right behind them. A tingle went along his spine as he wondered how much Manzetti had heard. But apparently he hadn't caught the substance of the conversation, for the only expression on his face was one of jocularity.

Joey said, "Oh, hi, Boss. Wan' you to meet a fren' of mine." He looked at Horton. "Wha's your name again?"

"Malone," Horton said. "Jimmy Malone."

Manzetti regarded him affably. Instead of offering his hand, he gave Horton's shoulder a friendly slap. "How are you, Jimmy? What you been feeding my boy to get him talking so hard?"

"Nothing," Horton said with a smile. "We're just batting the breeze."

"You new around here?" The question was merely polite, not curious.

"About a month. I've been here before. Matter of fact, you've bought me a couple of drinks, but you wouldn't remember it."

Manzetti grinned. "If I remembered all the guys I've bought drinks, I'd need a head like an elephant. Where you work?"

"Gotham's," Horton said, picking the name of a brewery he had passed on the way to the club. "Drive a truck."

"Yeah? Good beer." He called to one of the bartenders, "Hey, Henry! Give Joey and his pal Jimmy a drink."

He gave Horton's shoulder another friendly pat and moved on.

Horton made no attempt to steer the conversation back to its former subject. He'd found what he wanted to know. Unless Joey was deliberately lying, which in his condition seemed unlikely, Manzetti was not only innocent of Quincy's murder, but of sending the threatening note, too.

Joey had forgotten what he had been talking about. He started another joke. Horton listened patiently while he sipped the beer Manzetti had bought. He finished it just as Joey finished the story.

"I better be pushing," Horton said. "Got to work tomorrow."

Joey looked a trifle blearily at the clock over the backbar. "Almos' midnight," he said with surprise. "Gonna close anyway. Which way you go?"

"To the Palais Royal."

"Run you home. Gotta car outside."

Horton wasn't enthusiastic about riding with a drunk, but he wasn't keen on a two-mile walk after all the beer he'd consumed either. Besides, there was no way to refuse the invitation without offending the man.

"Fine," he said, trying to make it sound appreciative.

As they started toward the door together, they ran into Tony Manzetti.

"Taking off before we close?" he asked Horton. Then he glanced at Joey. "Where you going?"

"Run Jimmy home," Joey said.

Manzetti looked surprised. "You sure got my boy wound up," he said to Horton. "Never saw him so friendly."

Throwing an arm across the shoulder of each man, he escorted them to the door and out into the hall. "Don't worry about Joey's driving," he told Horton. "He's a better driver drunk than most guys sober."

"Glad of that," Horton said with a feeling of relief.

Then his relief changed to consternation. The street door opened and a young man came in alone.

He said, "Hi, Tony. Still time for a nightcap?"

Then his gaze fell on Horton and his eyes widened.

"Hey!" he said. "You're the guy I sold that car! The guy who killed Mr. Quincy!"

It was the young salesman from Trusting Joe Gannon's used-car lot.

CHAPTER XIII

Horton didn't wait for Manzetti and Joey to react. Leaping forward, he stiff-armed the young salesman out of the way and clawed at the handle of the street door.

But even drunk, Joey Ault's co-ordination was excellent. He was moving only an instant after Horton. As Horton started to jerk the door open, a pistol barrel descended on the back of his head.

The blow didn't knock him out. It just drove him to his knees with his senses reeling. His forehead butted against the half-open door and slammed it shut. He stayed on his knees, his palms pressed against the door, conscious but momentarily paralyzed.

He heard Manzetti growl something, then he was jerked to his feet by Manzetti on one side and Joey on the other.

"You!" Manzetti snapped at the young car salesman. "Get in the bar, and clam up about this. I'll talk to you later."

Horton didn't see whether or not the young man complied. He was pushed past him in the direction of the stairs before the salesman could turn to enter the bar.

Still so numb that his legs refused to work properly, Horton stumbled up the stairway with Manzetti and Joey supporting him on either side. They reached the dark second floor and turned down a pitch-black hallway. Suddenly Horton was thrust forward, and sensed rather than saw the doorway he was being pushed through. His arms were released and he fell to his hands and knees in the darkness. Groggily, he raised his head just as the room lights came on.

After a moment Horton's head cleared enough for him to rise shakily to his feet. He closed his eyes against the light as blinding pain struck the base of his skull. When the pain finally subsided to a dull ache, he opened them again.

They were in a small office. Horton moved unsteadily to a chair against one wall and sat down. Manzetti closed and locked the office door.

Joey the Cut, a forty-five automatic in his hand, was glaring at Horton and breathing heavily. When he spoke, all thickness had left his voice.

Apparently he was one of those rare people who can sober instantly in emergency.

"You was pumping me," he spat at Horton. "All that friendly stuff was just bull to make me talk."

He stepped forward with his gun barrel raised, as though he meant to smash it across Horton's face.

"Hold it, Joey!" Manzetti's voice cracked out.

With an effort, the hatchet man restrained himself from completing the movement. His hand slowly lowered until the gun muzzle pointed between Horton's eyes. He backed a step, keeping his eyes fixed on Horton's. His lips drew back in an animal-like grimace.

Manzetti walked over to Horton and jerked the cap from his head.

"You answer the description, all right, mister." He flung the cap at Horton's chest and it rolled down into his lap. "What you doing around here?"

Gingerly Horton touched the back of his head. His cap had deadened the force of Joey's blow, but it had still been a substantial rap. A bump was beginning to form.

He said wearily, "Just trying to clear myself of a bum beef."

"Yeah? By setting me up to take it for you?"

Horton started to shake his head, thought better of it when he felt a twinge of pain. "I didn't kill Quincy," he said. "I was in the washroom when somebody opened the outside door and fired. I ran because the cops would never have believed me."

"Sure," Manzetti said. "But you think I will."

"It's the truth," Horton insisted. "Why do you think I came here tonight?"

"You tell me."

"I was hoping to find evidence that you ordered him killed," Horton said sullenly. "Would I do that if I knew I'd killed him?"

"So you *were* trying to set me up, hull?"

"Only if you were guilty. After talking to Joey, I was satisfied you weren't. If you'd let me walk out, I wouldn't have bothered you any more."

"Glad you're convinced I'm clean," Manzetti said ironically. "Now convince me that you are."

"Why would I kill the guy?" Horton asked. "I had him all set up for a bunco score. The killing ruined all my plans."

"Yeah? What were your plans?"

Horton told him. There was nothing to be gained in holding back, and possibly some advantage if he could get Manzetti to believe the truth. He outlined the bunco game he had been in the process of working in detail.

He finished by saying, "So you see, Quincy was doing exactly what I wanted. I wouldn't have killed him to avoid arrest, as the cops seem to think. I *wanted* to be arrested. And I certainly wasn't hired to gun him by Mrs. Quincy, as you seem to think. I never saw her until a few minutes before Quincy died. She was in the office when I arrived, but left immediately after."

Manzetti said sharply, "What was that? She was there?"

"Sure. But she left."

"Well, well," Manzetti said thoughtfully. "And she told the cops she never left home that day."

Horton hiked his eyebrows. "That wasn't in the papers."

Manzetti gave him a wolfish grin. "I get my information direct. A lot of stuff never gets in the papers." He looked at Joey. "Could be this guy's telling the truth, Joey. Maybe Velda Quincy pulled the kill all by herself. And Jimmy-boy was just unlucky enough to get caught in the middle."

Joey made no response. He merely continued to stare at Horton with hate.

"Of course I'm telling the truth," Horton urged. "You ever hear of a con man using a gun?"

Manzetti studied him estimatingly. "No, as a matter of fact. But you know what? If you can convince me you're innocent, maybe the cops would buy your story too."

Horton looked at him doubtfully.

"And where would that leave me?" Manzetti inquired. "The papers would start harping on that threat again as the probable motive. Even if the cops eventually pinned it on Velda, and proved she sent the note in order to let me take the rap, it would be a lot of trouble. And maybe they couldn't prove it."

"They wouldn't try very hard to prove it on you, would they?" Horton said.

"Not the cops," Manzetti told him with a slow shake of his head. "Not with the fix I've got. But the newspapers would play it to the hilt. It ain't good to have newspaper campaigns stirring things up."

"Then you're not going to turn me over to the police?" Horton asked hopefully.

Manzetti shook his head again. "Don't believe I will."

Crossing to a desk in one corner, he lifted a phone and dialled. After a moment, he said, "Henry? Any of the boys still in the bar?"

There was a pause, then, "Okay. Send Hippo and Russ up to my office."

As Manzetti replaced the phone in its cradle, Horton stood up. "All right if I run along, then?"

Manzetti regarded him without expression. "We wouldn't want you to be lonesome. You can ride home with Joey and a couple of the other boys."

Joey removed his smoldering gaze from Horton long enough to glance at Manzetti. "What's the pitch, Boss?"

"We'll wind this up nice and clean, Joey. I like the theory the cops have got now. Why bother them with a lot of complicated stuff about Quincy's widow? It's no skin off our noses if she gets away with murder."

Horton said uneasily, "What are you getting at, Manzetti?"

Manzetti ignored him. He said to Joey, "Know where Jimmy-boy's hideout is?"

"He said the Palais Royal."

"Good. That's a nice quiet place. Arrange it to look natural."

"Arrange what?" Horton inquired loudly.

"Your suicide," Manzetti told him with a calmness approaching indifference. "Nothing like a suicide to wind up a murder case neat. About the most convincing confession of guilt there is."

CHAPTER XIV

A knock came at the door and Manzetti moved to unlock it. Two men came in.

It wasn't difficult to guess which one was Hippo and which Russ. One was grossly fat, with a round face and unblinking little eyes. The other was a lean, wiry man with blond hair carefully set in waves.

Neither said anything. After a glance at Horton, they merely looked inquiringly at Manzetti.

"This is the joker the cops want for knocking over Honest John Quincy," Manzetti said, nodding toward Horton. "We're going to let him confess by bumping himself off. Joey will give you the details."

Both men gave understanding nods. For all the change in expression either exhibited, Manzetti might have been detailing them to run to the corner for a package of cigarettes.

Joey said, "All right, mister. Get going." He gestured toward the door with his gun.

They went down the stairs in single file. The tat Hippo went first, then Horton, then Joey, his gun pocketed but pointing at Horton's back through the cloth. Russ and Manzetti brought up the rear.

The barroom was now closed. As they passed the open doorway, Horton could see the three bartenders cleaning up, and the only remaining customer, the young car salesman, patiently waiting at the bar as Manzetti had ordered.

Manzetti dropped out of the parade. Without saying anything, he turned into the barroom.

Joey and Russ waited at the curb with Horton while Hippo brought around a car. Neither said anything to him.

Horton, who was carrying his cap in his hand, started to raise it to put it on. Joey's eyes glittered at the movement, and a fleeting expression of eagerness crossed his face. Horton carefully dropped his hand to his side again. The thin killer was so impatient to put a bullet in him, any movement at all was dangerous.

Hippo pulled up to the curb in a two-year-old, black Buick sedan. Joey urged Horton into the back seat, waited until Russ sat next to him and covered him with a thirty-eight revolver, then rounded the car and sat on his other side. Horton, still afraid to make any unnecessary move-ment, let his cap lie in his lap.

Joey said, "Palais Royal, Hippo. Park on the sidestreet."

The two-mile trip was made in total silence. When they reached the hotel, Hippo swung the Buick right into the street alongside the building, made a U-turn and parked just back from the corner, out of sight of the front entrance.

Joey said to Russ, "Cover him," put away his own gun and got out of the car.

"Where you going?" Russ asked.

Through the open window Joey said, "Gonna find out the guy's room number and figure out how to get him in without passing the desk."

He moved off around the corner to the front of the hotel.

Hippo fumbled in his coat pocket for a package of cigarettes, stuck one in his mouth. Over his shoulder he said to Russ, "Got any fire?"

Russ felt in a pocket with his left hand. His gaze remained on Hor-ton, but momentarily the gun muzzle strayed forward.

It wasn't much of a chance, but it was the best one Horton was likely to get. He slashed the cap he was holding in his lap at Russ's eyes.

He was gripping the cap by its rear. The edge of the stiff, cardboard-reinforced peak caught the man directly between the eyes. He let out a startled yelp.

At the same instant that he swung the cap, Horton's left hand made a grab for the blond man's revolver. His fingers clamped over the cylinder, making it impossible for it to revolve and preventing it from firing.

Releasing his grip on the cap, Horton brought the edge of his palm sharply down on the man's wrist. Russ's fingers spasmodically opened. Both hands flew to his injured eyes as he cowered against the car door.

For a fat man, Hippo was well co-ordinated. The second he heard his partner's yelp, he was twisting around in the front seat and driving a hand toward his armpit. He was on one knee facing rearward, his gun swinging toward Horton, just as Horton jerked the revolver from Russ's grip.

There wasn't time for Horton to transfer the gun to his right hand. Still holding it around the cylinder, he slashed upward with it.

The wooden grip caught Hippo flush on the point of the chin with such force it made Horton's hand tingle. The fat man's small eyes blink-ed and he fell sidewise, face down on the front seat. Transferring the .38 butt-first to his right hand, Horton swung it in an arc to crash against Russ's forehead. The blond man collapsed without a sound.

Leaning over Russ, Horton opened the door and pushed his uncon-scious figure out onto the sidewalk. He scrambled out the same door, slammed it and jerked open the front one. With his pistol raised to strike downward, he waited for some movement from Hippo. There was none. The man was as unconscious as Russ.

Thrusting the .38 into his jacket pocket, Horton grasped the fat man by his shoulders and heaved him onto the sidewalk too.

He was behind the wheel and had the motor started when Joey appeared from around the corner of the hotel on his way back to the car.

Joey took one look and reached for his gun. Horton shot the Buick forward and made a dirt-track left turn onto Gibbons Street.

A single shot sounded. A webbed hole appeared in the right side of the windshield as the bullet zipped through the rear window and out the front. Then he was out of pistol range, his right foot to the floorboards.

Horton headed straight for the center of town, his only immediate thought to put as much distance as possible between himself and Manzetti's men. As he drove, his mind was working at full speed, considering his situation.

It was unlikely that Manzetti would set the police on his trail, he decided, for the racketeer didn't want him to fall into their hands alive. His simple disguise was probably still good insofar as the police were concerned.

But Manzetti had a substantial organization of his own which would now be hunting for him. The evening's activities had increased the precariousness of his position even more, he thought ruefully. Now not only the police were after him, but a whole corps of hired killers as well.

The first thing he had to do was get rid of the Buick, as undoubtedly Manzetti's men would be out looking for it. He slowed, considering a place to abandon it where it wouldn't be spotted immediately.

By now he was well downtown. Just ahead was Honest John Quincy's used-car lot. He started to drive slowly past it, then, on an impulse, halted the car and thoughtfully examined the lot.

At this time of night it was deserted. A string of white bulbs encircling the lot lighted it brilliantly.

Horton glanced in all directions. At the moment there was neither a pedestrian nor an automobile in sight.

Swinging the car onto the lot, he found a vacant place in one of the rows of cars and backed into it. It would be at least morning before anyone discovered the car there, and possibly, if one of the salesmen didn't notice it among all the other cars, it might even be days. In any event it was unlikely that any of Manzetti's men would spot it before he was well out of the neighborhood.

His cap now constituted more of an identifying mark than it did a disguise.

A block from where he had abandoned the car he dropped the cap into a trash can.

Sticking to sidestreets, Horton put eight blocks between himself and the car. Finally he came to a small, dimly-lighted park. Following a footpath, he found a bench shadowed by a tree and out of sight of the street. He sank onto the bench, lit a cigarette and considered his next move.

Due to his unfortunate habit of carrying only a small amount of money with him, he had less than twenty dollars on his person. The rest, and his traveler's checks, was in his room. It would be suicide to attempt to get past Manzetti's men to his room.

He could, of course, call on Belle or the colonel for a loan, but he hated to do it. Money wasn't his worst problem anyway. It was time. He had to prove his innocence before either Manzetti or the police caught up with him.

Horton was now thoroughly satisfied that Manzetti was not responsible for Quincy's death. The performances of both Manzetti himself and of Joey the Cut had been too convincing. The most likely murder suspect was the blonde Velda.

There remained the problem of how to prove she was guilty, or even how to start an investigation. If he tried to visit the woman, she'd probably yell for the police.

His thoughts turned to the red-haired Helen Quincy. She had seemed to dislike Velda so intensely, perhaps she would be willing to help.

He wondered if Helen would give him a chance to explain himself before calling the police, if he attempted to contact her. At the time she had warned him that police were coming to his room, she couldn't have known what they wanted with him. She might not be nearly so co-operative now that the papers had announced he was wanted for murder. The murder of her step-father at that.

Still, she had obviously liked him a great deal. And she had covered for him when he fled from the Lawford. Contacting her would be risky, but he could think of no other logical move.

He decided that if he was going to get in touch with Helen Quincy, he had to do it at once, even though it was now past one A.M. By morning the news that his record had arrived from St. Louis would be in all the papers. It was going to be hard enough to talk Helen into trusting him, without having to explain a long record as a confidence man.

Stepping on his cigarette, he rose from the bench and left the park in search of a phone booth.

CHAPTER XV

At an all-night drugstore Horton unobtrusively slid into a phone booth and opened the telephone directory. The only Quincy listed was the dead man.

Horton frowned. It seemed unlikely, in view of Helen's dislike of Velda, that she had lived at her step-father's home. Then a thought struck him. Many hotels provided their desk employees room as part of their pay. It was quite possible that Helen lived right at the Lawford.

Dropping a coin, he dialed the Lawford's number. When the switchboard answered, he said in a confident tone, "Will you ring Miss Helen Quincy's room, please?"

Then he held his breath. But apparently he had guessed correctly. His only answer was the sound of a phone ringing.

After three rings, a sleepy feminine voice said, "Yes?"

"Helen?" he asked.

He heard an indrawn breath as she recognized his voice.

"Don't be upset," he said rapidly. "And please don't hang up." He paused, then said, "Switchboard operator!"

The operator's voice said, "Yes, sir?"

He was thankful that he had taken the precaution. At this time of night the board would be so inactive, probably the operator left the line open on all calls out of sheer boredom.

"I don't want this call monitored," he said. "Will you please close your line?"

"Certainly, sir," she said in an offended voice.

Horton hoped the telephone company rule applied to hotel switchboards. He knew that a long-distance operator who eavesdropped on a conversation after being asked not to monitor the call was subject to instant dismissal. He had no idea if the same rule applied to other operators, but he had to chance that it did.

Helen said, "What do you want?"

"Your belief, first," he said. "I didn't do what the papers said. Nothing you read is true. Do you believe me?"

"I haven't known what to think," she said slowly.

"Will you give me a chance to explain?" he asked. "I think I know who did do it, and I need your help. I want to see you."

When she made no immediate reply, he said, "I know I sound crazy. You don't owe me anything, and for all I know, you'll walk me right into a police trap. But I have to chance it. Will you see me?"

"Tonight?" she asked. "It's past one."

"It has to be tonight. Tomorrow will be too late. Believe me, I wouldn't bother you at this time of night if it wasn't urgent."

There was a moment of silence as she thought things over. Then she said, "Where do you want to see me?"

"Any place public would be too dangerous," he said. "And I haven't a room. Or rather, I have one I can't use. It's staked out by Manzetti's men."

"Manzetti?" she said, startled. "Tony Manzetti?"

"Yeah. It's a long story, but he's after me as well as the police. I'll explain it all when I see you. Is there any way you can get me into the hotel without anyone seeing me?"

After another moment of silence, she said, "The service door. There won't be anyone in the kitchen now. How soon will you be?"

"Twenty minutes, probably. I'm about a mile from there, and I'm walking. I'll have to take a kind of roundabout route to miss the main streets."

"All right," she said. "Go up the alley behind the hotel. There's a light over the service entrance. I'll be waiting in the kitchen."

It took Horton the full twenty minutes he had estimated to traverse the mile. And for most of the distance his heart was in his throat.

With the bars closed for more than an hour, the streets were practically deserted. He was therefore a pretty conspicuous target for anyone who might be searching for him. Once a car slowed just as it passed him, and his fingers tightened around his gun butt. It must not have been any of Manzetti's men, though, for it picked up speed and moved on.

At an intersection, a police radio car came to a dead stop right alongside him. He tensed to start running, then realized just in time that it had halted for a boulevard stop sign. It moved on with only a casual glance from one of the uniformed officers in the front seat.

After that Horton moved through as many alleys as he could find. When he finally reached the Hotel Lawford, his zig-zag route had nearly doubled the mile distance from his starting point.

He was like the crooked man in the Mother Goose rhyme, he thought. *There was a crooked man, and he walked a crooked mile. He found a crooked sixpence against a crooked stile.*

He mused ironically that the rhyme symbolized his whole life. By the standards of society he was certainly a crooked man. And he had chosen his own crooked road to walk.

At the mouth of the alley behind the Lawford he studied the shadows suspiciously. If Helen had phoned the police, here was where they probably would be waiting for him. Nothing happened, however, as he approached the green-shaded light over a door in the center of the building.

A soft rap on the door, it immediately opened and he stepped inside. Helen quietly pushed the door closed again and dropped a bar in place.

There was only a night light on in the kitchen, but it was bright enough for him to see the girl quite clearly. He noted that she had not only dressed since his call, but had gone to considerable trouble to make herself attractive. Her red hair was carefully brushed and her mouth freshly painted. Horton had a habit of close observation where women were concerned. He noticed that she had even mascaraed her eyelashes.

He felt a touch of relief. Apparently his charm was still working on the girl. It wasn't likely that a woman would carefully primp herself for a man's visit if she only expected to turn him over to the police.

Then he became aware that her charm was still working on him, too. She had colored slightly under his observation, and he found himself grinning with delight at this lack of sophistication. Horton wasn't used to women still fresh enough to blush.

Fingering his day-old beard, he said, "You make me feel as though we're Beauty and the Beast. Forgive the stubble. It's part of my disguise."

Her return smile was shy and nervous. "Just follow me," she said in a low voice.

She led him out of the kitchen into a hall. Swinging, glass-topped doors across the hall gave onto the main dining room. Helen turned right to the open door of a freight elevator. She manipulated the controls to raise them to the seventh floor.

Horton got a mild shock when they stepped from the car. They were directly across the hall from Belle's room.

He breathed a little more easily when Helen led him down the hall, around a corner and the full length of that hall to another turn. Her room was on the opposite side of the hotel from Belle's.

They passed no one at all in the hallways. Helen slipped her key into the door of room 786.

Inside she pushed the door closed and emitted a sigh of relief.

"I'm glad that's over," she said. "Afraid I wouldn't make a very good gunman's moll. I get too nervous." Then she asked, "Would you like a drink?"

"If it's not beer," he told her. "I had about a month's quota of beer today."

Some of the rooms at the Lawford were equipped with refrigerators. Horton's had possessed one, and Helen's did too. Sliding back a wall panel, she disclosed its small door. When she opened it, Horton saw that it was well-stocked with beer and soda. She took out an ice tray and handed it to him.

"You fix the ice," she instructed. "You'll find a glass bowl in the bathroom."

It was the old-fashioned type of tray which had to have water run over it to get the cubes out. When Horton returned from the bathroom with the filled bowl, she had produced a bottle of bourbon and had poured a substantial amount into each of two glasses. She dropped cubes into them and looked at Horton inquiringly.

"Usually I take water," he said. "But I need a pickup. I'll just have it on the rocks."

She added a little soda to hers.

When they were seated with drinks and cigarettes, the girl on the bed and Horton in a chair next to it, she said, "Now I think I deserve the explanation you promised."

"You do that," he agreed. "Incidentally, I had to run out on my hotel bill. When this is over, I'll pay it."

Helen brushed this aside. "You're accused of murder, and you worry about a hotel bill. Let's stick to the important matters."

During the ride up on the freight elevator, Horton had mulled over the problem of just how much of the truth he should tell Helen. He had decided to make a clean breast of everything, including his bunco game, for it would be difficult to explain his reason for visiting her step-father's used-car lot if he didn't tell the truth. If he made up a lie and was disbelieved, Helen would automatically be convinced he was the murderer. On the other hand, he had already tested out the true story on Tony Manzetti and had found belief. He was fairly certain the girl would believe it, too.

In addition to this, he knew a woman would more readily forgive a man's sin when he confessed it than she would if she learned of it from an outside source. In the first case she had only the sin to forgive. In the second, she had to forgive both the sin and his deceit.

Horton said, "To start off, I wasn't trying to get your step-father to cash a bad check, as the papers said. I offered him a check in partial payment for a car, but there was nothing wrong with it. I have fifteen thousand dollars on deposit at Rice City National Bank."

Helen gave him a relieved smile. "I knew the papers couldn't be right. You just didn't look like a crook."

Horton took a gulp of his drink to steel himself for the plunge. Then he said, "I am though, Helen. Just not the type the papers said."

She frowned without understanding. "What?"

"I'm a bunco artist."

Helen looked confused. "A what?"

"A con man. I was trying to pull a confidence game on your step-father when he got killed."

She said slowly, "I don't think I understand."

He told her, outlining his plan for the third time, just as he had told it to Belle and Manzetti. As he described the gimmick, it occurred to him that if he continued to tell it to people, the idea would be useless for future use. It would spread all over the country by word of mouth.

By the time he reached the point of the story where her step-father was killed, Helen's expression was a mixture of shock and disapproval. But at least there was no suggestion of disbelief on her face.

Doggedly, he ploughed right on with a description of his activities after the murder, omitting nothing except mention of Belle's and the colonel's help. When he described his unmasking at the Sixth Ward Athletic Club and the subsequent attempt by Manzetti's men to kill him, her expression of disapproval faded to one of alarm. He didn't tell her of his suspicion of Velda. He wanted to save that until he had cleared the air by his confession and had gotten her back into a co-operative mood.

When he finished, there was a long silence. Then she said, "Why did you tell me this, Jim?"

"Because it's the truth."

"I mean, why did you want me to know?"

"A couple of reasons. I wanted to convince you I had no reason to kill your step-father. Have I convinced you?"

She gave a reluctant nod. "Yes, I believe you. But this other is something of a shock. I suppose it's the lesser of two evils to learn you're a confidence man instead of a killer, but it's still a shock. What's the other reason?"

"I simply didn't want to deceive you."

She thought this over, and a touch of color came to her cheeks again. She took a sip of her drink to cover her blush, and selfconsciously tapped ashes from her cigarette. "I suppose in a way that's flattering," she conceded. "But do you always do things like this? I mean, is that the way you make your living?"

He said, "I'm afraid it is, Helen."

CHAPTER XVI

Neither said anything for a time. They sipped their drinks, finished their cigarettes and stubbed them out. Helen sat with downcast eyes, thinking deeply.

Finally she looked up and asked, "Do you have a prison record?"

"No," he said. "I'm known to police in a number of places. Not wanted by them; just known."

"In other words, you're a successful confidence man?"

"You could put it that way," he admitted.

"Doesn't your conscience ever bother you?"

"Why should it?" he asked. "I don't fleece widows and orphans. I've never yet taken a man who couldn't afford the loss. And with taxes what they are today, it's all deductible."

"That sounds like rationalization," she said with disapproval.

"It is," he admitted. "Any way you look at it, I make a dishonest living. But compared to most bunco artists, I'm a paragon of virtue. The average con man wouldn't hesitate to take the last cent of a widow with seven children, and wouldn't lose a minute's sleep if he later heard they all starved to death. I confine myself to taking well-to-do businessmen."

"It's just as dishonest to cheat them as it is to cheat widows."

"Of course," he agreed. "I'll even admit my motive is selfish. I couldn't stand to have a starving widow on my conscience. Picking the type victims I do, I can sleep like a baby."

She considered him thoughtfully for a long time. Horton finished his drink, rose and set the empty glass on the dresser. She sipped the last of hers and held the empty glass for him to take.

"Another?" he asked.

She shook her head. "I'm trying to make up my mind about you."

"I know," he said. "Take your time." He set her glass on the dresser.

"You *were* truthful with me," she said. "I suppose I ought to credit you with that."

He smiled at her.

"And if you really only cheat well-to-do men, you aren't as bad as you could be."

He smiled again.

"You could cheat women very easily, you know. You have a way with them."

"Thank you, ma'am," he said formally. "I think you're wonderful too."

"Do you really?" she asked, her expression of disapproval disappearing entirely.

In answer he walked over to the bed and tilted up her chin with one hand. He looked down at her for a moment, then stooped and kissed her solidly on the mouth. She made no attempt to turn her head, but her lips were passive. When he straightened, she stared up at him thoughtfully.

She said, "I have a philosophy."

Still cupping her face with one hand, he asked, "About what?"

"I believe you can't hurt people before you meet them. I mean, what a man does before he meets a woman shouldn't offend her. And vice-versa. Your past is your own business. But after they meet, if they mean anything to each other, what each one does is the other one's business."

"Sounds fair," he said.

A little breathlessly she said, "So don't kiss me any more unless you promise you'll reform."

Dropping his hand from her chin, he studied her curiously. The remark coming from any other woman would have struck him as so childlike that it bordered on inanity. Coming from Helen, it struck him only as delightfully innocent.

To his own surprise, he heard himself saying, "I think I'd promise you anything, and mean it."

Then he dropped to the bed alongside her and took her in his arms. Her lips were no longer passive.

Gently he pressed her back onto the bed.

* * * *

A ringing telephone awakened Horton. For a moment he couldn't recall where he was. Then a head stirred on his bare shoulder and Helen sat up, clutching the sheet to her bosom. With her free hand she lifted the phone from the bedside table.

Horton could hear a male voice over the phone say, "It's eight o'clock, Miss Quincy."

Helen said, "Thank you," and hung up.

"My regular morning call," she said to Horton. "Close your eyes."

Obediently he closed them, then cheated by slitting them open again as she bounced from bed. He got a fleeting view of white flesh as she slipped into a robe.

The performance intrigued him. Last night she had at first delighted him with her fresh innocence, then startled him by her display of passion. Now her maidenly reserve in refusing to let him see her nakedness caused him fresh delight.

As she disappeared into the bathroom, he wondered if he had at last found the woman who would be worth waking up to every morning.

Helen wasn't due at work until nine. She explained allowing herself a full hour by telling Horton that she usually breakfasted at a restaurant a few blocks away, where the prices were more reasonable than the Lawford's. But this morning she would make an exception, she told him. She'd have breakfast sent up to the room.

She was showered and dressed for work by eight-fifteen. When Horton came from the bathroom fifteen minutes later, a waiter had already delivered breakfast and had departed.

Helen examined Horton's face with approval. "You found my razor, did you?" she asked.

"Uh-huh. Thanks."

She gave him a quick kiss on the cheek. "That's better. Last night you scratched. Now, let's eat." She grinned. "I ordered only one breakfast, but it's big enough for both of us."

On the breakfast cart there was orange juice, bacon and eggs, toast and coffee. They ate heartily, then lingered over their coffee.

Helen said, "That's more appetite than I usually have mornings. I wonder why?"

Horton merely cocked an eyebrow at her, and she blushed furiously. He laughed. "Don't ever change," he said.

"Change how?"

"Keep that split personality. You're a maiden and a wanton all rolled into one."

She colored again. "That's an awful thing to say."

"I meant it as a compliment," he told her. Then he hit his forehead. "You know, you distracted me so much, I completely forgot why I came here until now."

"I thought it was to confess."

"That was only part of it. Didn't I tell you over the phone that I thought I knew who the real killer was?"

For some reason she blushed again and averted her eyes.

"What's the matter?" he asked.

"I guess you did tell me," she said in a low voice. "You distracted me too. I never thought of it again until now."

He grinned at her, then sobered again. "Tony Manzetti's convinced it was Velda."

Helen looked at him wide-eyed. She didn't say anything.

"It's logical," Horton said. "Manzetti says he didn't send that threat. I believe him, because at the time he said it, he thought I was going to be dead before long. There wouldn't have been any point in lying."

Helen's brows puckered. "You think Velda put that note in the mailbox?"

"It figures. As Joey the Cut put it, Velda would know the first person the police look at when a man is murdered is his wife. But by planting a threatening note the day before she killed him, the finger would point to Manzetti. Everybody knew your step-father's committee was out to get Manzetti."

Helen said, "But why? What motive would she have?"

Horton raised his eyebrows. "Don't you know Velda's reputation?"

Helen shook her head. "What reputation? I don't like her, but I really don't know anything about her. Except I'm sure she married my step-father for his money."

Horton said incredulously, "You mean you've never heard the gossip? That Velda's a tramp? And your stepfather was getting ready to divorce her?"

Helen shook her head again.

"I suppose you wouldn't," Horton said after some thought. "People wouldn't repeat that sort of thing to a member of the family. Incidentally, if Quincy was so loaded with money, why do you have to work for a living?"

"We haven't gotten along since he met Velda," Helen said a little bitterly. "I moved out a year ago, when he married her. I haven't accepted any money from him since."

"Do you know if you're in his will?"

She shook her head. "I haven't the slightest idea."

"You're not being much help," he said disconsolately. "I thought maybe you could help me pin the killing on Velda. But I seem to know more about her than you do."

"I'm sorry," she said in a contrite voice. Then she brightened. "Maybe I *can* help you."

"How?"

"Wasn't the murder gun a forty-five automatic?"

"A forty-five. There's no way to tell whether it was an automatic or a revolver."

"Well, my step-father owned a forty-five automatic. If Velda killed him, she probably used that. Don't they have ways to tell that a certain gun was used?"

"Yeah. Ballistics tests."

"He kept it in the top drawer of his dresser, under some handkerchiefs. If Velda used it, then put it back in the same place, it would be proof of your innocence."

"Yeah," he said slowly. "If she was that foolish."

"At least it's a chance," she said. "Couldn't we phone an anonymous tip to the police, telling them to search for it?"

He grinned at her. "Now you're beginning to sound like a gun moll."

"I'm beginning to feel like one." She glanced at her watch. "I have to go to work. Do you want to hide here today? I'll be back up at noon, and can order some lunch sent up."

"I'll stay around awhile," he said. "I'll call you at the desk if I decide to leave."

"Wouldn't that be dangerous? Where would you go?"

"I may not go anywhere. I said *if.*"

He walked her to the door and gave her a good-by kiss. He felt a little like an unemployed husband sending his wife off to work.

CHAPTER XVII

Horton pushed the breakfast cart into the hall. He hung a "Do not disturb" sign on the doorknob in order to keep the cleaning maid from walking in on him.

For a time he sat smoking and thinking about his next move. Finally he lifted the phone and asked for room 727.

Belle answered in a sleepy voice. Apparently she was still in bed.

"Good morning," Horton said. "Wake you up?"

Immediately, she came wide awake. "Yes, but it's time I'm up. I've been worried about you. The colonel told me what you planned to do last night. Where are you?"

Horton said, "Not far away. Unlock your door. I'll be along in a couple of minutes."

"You're in the hotel?" she asked with surprise.

"Yeah. Be right there."

Hanging up, he cracked open the door and glanced both ways along the hall. A waiter was wheeling the empty breakfast cart toward the elevators. He waited until the man had pushed it onto a car and the elevator door closed.

Then he removed the "Do not disturb" sign and pushed the door closed from outside. He left it unlocked, in case he wanted to get back in. He walked quickly down the hall in the opposite direction from the passenger elevators.

Halfway down the second corridor, a middle-aged woman stepped from a room and moved past him on the way to the front elevators. She gave him only a cursory glance.

He encountered no one else. Belle's door was unlocked. He stepped into the room, lifted the "Do not disturb" sign from the inner knob and hung it on the outer one. Pushing the door shut, he clicked the lock.

In the bathroom he could hear the shower running. He lit a cigarette and waited.

Five minutes later, Belle appeared wrapped in a white satin robe. Her dark hair was pinned into a mass on top of her head, and her face without makeup was fresh and scrubbed-looking.

She said, "Don't you dare look at me," and scooted to the dresser to remove underthings from a drawer.

Belle possessed none of Helen's old-fashioned modesty. Casually she slipped from her robe, tossed it on the bed and began dressing. Horton watched with interest as she drew on flimsy panties, hooked on a bra and snapped a garter belt into place.

She glanced up at him as she drew on filmy stockings, and made a face. "Still playing Peeping Tom, aren't you?"

Horton grinned. "You make such nice peeping."

She stepped into high-heeled pumps, pulled a flowered street dress over her head, turned her back to him and said, "Zip, please."

He pulled up the rear zipper.

Turning around, she said, "Now that I'm decent, you may kiss me good morning before I apply the paint."

Bending, he gave her a casual peck. She cocked an eyebrow at him.

"Am I that unappetizing without makeup? Or have you found another woman?"

She meant it as a joke, but it was such an accurate guess, he suddenly felt guilty. It must have showed in his face, because her eyes narrowed.

"You have been two-timing me, haven't you?" she accused. "And you've only been out of my sight for forty hours."

"Has it been that long?" he asked with surprise.

"I've been counting them. The passage of time wouldn't be as important to you. You're not in love."

Swinging her back to him, she seated herself at the dressing table and began to make up her face. She used nothing but a touch of powder and bright lipstick. Her eyebrows and lashes were dark enough not to require mascara.

Then she unpinned her hair and began to brush it with long, even strokes.

"Who is she?" she asked suddenly.

"Who?" he hedged.

"The woman you've been with?"

He walked over to the dressing table and stubbed out his cigarette in a tray lying there. He looked down at her thoughtfully.

Glancing up, she said, "Know something funny?"

"What?"

"You're probably the top bunco artist in the business. Your trade is fooling people. Probably nobody else in the world could read your thoughts, if you wanted to conceal them. Not even Dunninger. But I can always sense what you're thinking as easily as though your head were made of glass."

"You read me because we're kindred souls."

She returned to her brushing. "Make a joke of it. I suppose I deserve it. It's really none of my business what women you tomcat around with."

He leaned down and brushed her cheek with his lips. "Stop trying to make me feel like a heel, Belle. You've succeeded. Isn't that enough?"

The brush halted its rhythmic movement and her hand fell to her lap. She turned her head to look up into his face.

"I'm sorry," she said. "I sound like a jealous vixen. Before I ever let myself fall in love with you, I knew you'd never be satisfied with only one woman. I just didn't think it would be so soon. Is she nice?"

"Do we have to talk about it?" he asked.

"No, of course not." She resumed her brushing. "Let's talk about your problem. Did you visit that club the colonel told you about?"

"Yes."

"Learn anything?"

"Quite a lot. And nearly got myself killed."

She gave him a startled look. "Really?"

"Really," he assured her. He told her everything that had happened at the Sixth Ward Athletic Club and afterward, up to the time he escaped in the Buick.

Belle said, "So now you're not only hiding from the police, but from Manzetti's men."

"Yeah," he said. "I seem to have everybody mad at me but you and the colonel."

She laid down the brush, examined her gleaming hair in the mirror and seemed satisfied.

"Forgive me for returning to a subject that's supposed to be tabled," she said. "But as busy as you've been, when did you find time to sandwich in the mysterious other woman? After you escaped from Manzetti's men?"

"I didn't have anyplace to go. I couldn't return to the Palais Royal. She was kind enough to hide me out for the night."

"Just like that?" she asked incredulously. "Where did you meet her? On the street?"

"I already knew her," he said patiently. "I phoned her at one o'clock in the morning."

"Oh. I forgot that you'd been in town a full twenty-four hours before the murder. Naturally you'd have a number of alternate women lined up in that time. It was silly of me to ask."

He said tiredly, "Will you stop it, Belle? Do you want me to go?"

Instantly she became contrite. Laying a hand on his arm, she said, "I really am sorry, Jim. I promise I'll control my jealousy. What are your plans now? And how can I help?"

He studied her face, saw that she meant it and smiled at her. "First I need a change of disguise. Since Manzetti's hirelings will be looking for someone dressed as a bum, I thought I'd turn gentleman again. I'll just have to take a chance on being recognized by the police."

"Isn't that a dangerous chance?" she asked dubiously.

"Not as dangerous as letting Manzetti's goons spot me. At least the police aren't out to kill me. They'll leave that to the state. There's a sport coat and a pair of slacks in the suitcase you have here. If you would go out and buy me a hat to hide my scrub-brush hair, I think I can get by. I'll need some fresh underclothes, socks and a shirt, too. All I own are at the Palais Royal."

He took out his wallet and handed her a ten-dollar bill. It left him a five and three ones.

"About a size seven hat?" she asked.

"Yes." He gave her the sizes of the other items.

"Then what do you plan to do?" she asked. "Visit this Velda woman?"

"I'd like a look at the inside of her house. I'll need the colonel's help to lure her away. Why don't you call him and ask him to come over here while you're shopping?"

"All right." She went to the phone and called the Rafferty House.

When she had the colonel on the line, she said, "Our friend would like to see you. Here at my room. I'll be out, so use the code knock."

When she hung up, she said to Horton, "He'll be over in twenty minutes. Don't open the door until you hear a quick double knock, followed by a pause and a single one. Otherwise it might be the cleaning woman."

Belle told him not to expect her back for an hour, as she'd have breakfast while she was out.

At the door she hesitated for a moment, then decided to offer her cheek for a good-by kiss. When he bent to touch it with his lips, her fingers squeezed his forearm.

"Don't let my jealousy upset you," she said. "I told you I don't expect reciprocation. Nothing has changed so far as I'm concerned. I'll still do anything I can to help you out of this mess."

She gave his arm another squeeze, pulled open the door, and was gone.

CHAPTER XVIII

Colonel Bob Desmond arrived twenty-five minutes later. At the sound of his code knock, Horton let him in and bolted the door again.

The colonel surveyed him through his invisible monocle. "You've shaved," he said in a disappointed tone.

While waiting, Horton had gotten a light plaid sport coat and a pair of gray slacks from the suitcase Belle was holding for him, and had laid them on the bed. He pointed to them.

"I'm going to spoil your kick altogether," he said. "I'm discarding my unpressed trousers and worn jacket for those as soon as Belle returns with the accessories."

"Seems a shame," the colonel said. "You made such a convincing bum. Aren't you afraid the police will spot you in that outfit?"

Horton explained the reason for the change. Briefly he described his previous night's activities.

Then he said, "I'd like a look at the inside of Velda's house. If she used her husband's forty-five, maybe she didn't dispose of it afterward. If I could find it and get a sample slug fired from it—"

"You mean fire it right inside the house?" the colonel interrupted. His right eyebrow climbed and his left eye squinted nearly closed.

"Depends on the circumstances," Horton said. "How far away other houses are, whether I can find something to fire it into which will preserve the slug. I may have to take the gun away to test it, then plant it back where I found it later."

"Hmm. Suppose the woman's home?"

"That's where you come in," Horton told him. "With your assignment to write up the murder, it would be perfectly logical for you to interview the widow. I want you to invite her out to lunch."

Colonel Bob looked astonished. "You fancy that she'd accept? So soon after becoming a widow? According to this morning's paper, the funeral isn't even till tomorrow."

"If all the things I've heard about her are true, that shouldn't deter her. Make your voice over the phone sound virile, so she won't suspect you're such a broken-down old wreck."

The colonel drew his already erect figure even straighter. "I haven't had any complaints from women yet, my good fellow. Don't let my lack of hair fool you. There's still plenty on my chest."

Horton grinned at him. "Better get moving. It's ten now. Try to get her to meet you somewhere for lunch at one. You can phone me here to let me know if you succeeded."

* * * *

About a half hour after the colonel departed, Belle returned laden with packages.

"I got everything," she said. "But it exhausted your ten. I only made it by settling for a two-ninety-five hat at Penney's. It looks all right, though."

Horton stripped and reclothed himself from the skin outward. When he was redressed, he surveyed himself in the full-length mirror of the bathroom door.

Again he was the well-dressed man from head to toe. Even his shoes were polished, as he had exchanged the ones he had dulled for a pair of brown brogans in his suitcase. The brown, snap-brim hat Belle had purchased concealed his crew cut as effectively as the cap had, and even made his ears less apparent. He decided that with a measure of luck, he might even pass the scrutiny of police.

Belle said, "I like you better as the executive type than I do as a truck driver."

Horton transferred the thirty-eight revolver from his jacket pocket to the right pocket of the sport coat, then doubtfully studied the bulge it made.

"It's pretty obvious," Belle told him.

He removed the gun and tossed it on the bed. "Hide it away some-where, will you, Belle? I don't think I could shoot anyone anyway."

She picked it up and put it under some underthings in a dresser drawer.

A few minutes later the colonel phoned. Belle answered, then passed the phone to Horton.

"No trouble at all, my good fellow," the colonel boomed. "When she heard my deep, masculine voice, she literally cooed. We're to meet at a place called the River-glade Inn at one. You should have a clear field from then until at least two-thirty."

"Thanks," Horton told him.

When he hung up, he glanced at his watch and saw that it was nearly eleven.

"I need a car," he said to Belle. "Want to do me another favor?"

"Of course."

"There's a car-rental agency just up the sreet. Harrod's U-Drive Service. Could you rent me something in your name?"

"All right."

"I'll have to owe you. My money's all at the Palais Royal."

"Why didn't you say so?" she asked. "Want some extra money?"

He shook his head. "The car's all I need."

Belle left him alone again. It was nearly noon when she finally came back. She handed him a set of car keys.

"It's parked on the north side of the hotel," she said. "A 1958 Ford sedan. Blue and white."

"Thanks a million, Belle. You've been wonderful. When this is all over, I'll make it up to you." He glanced at his watch again. "I have to go now."

At the door she clung to him for a moment. "Be careful," she said. "When will I see you again?"

"I'll phone you," he told her.

Out in the hall, he turned in the direction of Helen's room with the intention of calling her from there in order to keep his promise to inform her if he decided to leave the hotel. He found her door locked. Apparently the cleaning maid had been there and had locked it when she left.

As he stood there undecided as to what to do, one of the elevator doors up the hall opened. Horton was turning to walk unobtrusively back the way he had come when he saw Helen step from the car alone. Halting his movement, he waited for her.

Helen regarded his new outfit with astonishment. Horton waited until she had keyed open the door and they were inside the room before offering any explanation.

Then he said, "I had a friend here at the hotel storing some of my clothes."

"A woman friend?" she asked quickly.

Horton felt a little hemmed in. He was beginning to get tired of female jealousy.

"Yes," he said flatly, and let it lie there.

After a moment, when it became apparent he had no intention of elaborating, she said a trifle lamely, "I see. Shall I order some lunch sent up?"

"I won't have time to wait," he said. "I have to be out to Velda's home shortly after one. I'll catch a sandwich somewhere en route."

"You're going to see her?" Helen asked, wide-eyed.

"She won't be there. I've arranged for a friend to lure her away for a time. I just want a look at your step-father's gun, if it's still in the house."

"You intend to break in?"

"Yes."

Crossing to the dresser, she opened the top drawer and took out a pair of keys on a chain. She removed one key and handed it to him.

"I never gave back my keys when I moved out," she said. "This will save you some trouble. It's to the front door."

"Thanks," he said, pocketing it. "I'll get it back to you."

"Do be careful, will you, Jim?"

He grinned at her. "Do I worry you?"

"You know you do." She moved against him and laid her head on his chest. "I don't want anything to happen to you."

"I'll try to stay out of the clutches of both the police and Manzetti," he said, giving her back a comforting pat.

Turning up her face, she offered her lips. He touched them gently with his, then drew her to him when he felt them part. Her arms flew about his neck and tightened.

After a moment he reluctantly pushed her away. "Any more of that and I won't leave."

She stood with her hands clasped in front of her like a little girl, her expression a trifle lost. "Will you call me?" she asked.

"Of course."

He was opening the door when she said, "How are you going to get out of the hotel? One of the elevator operators might recognize you."

"Walk down."

"Seven floors? Let me take you down in the freight elevator. From the lower hall you can get to the side entrance without being seen from the lobby."

"All right," he agreed.

They passed no one on the way to the freight elevator. The indicator showed that it was on first, and Horton felt a trifle uneasy as they waited for it to rise. The closed door to Belle's room was right behind them.

He breathed a sigh of relief when the elevator door finally opened. Then, as they stepped into the car, Belle's door suddenly opened. Belle was dressed for the street, wearing a hat and carrying a purse. She halted in the doorway and her eyes moved from Horton to Helen.

Helen touched the controls and the door slid shut. Horton's last view of Belle was of her staring at Helen with an air of deliberate appraisal.

Helen was unconscious of the appraisal, or even of Belle's presence. Her attention was centered on the elevator controls.

CHAPTER XIX

Horton had no difficulty locating the Ford Belle had rented. He drove a few blocks north, then stopped at a busy hamburger stand for a sandwich and a cup of coffee.

This was his first test of his new "disguise" in public, and he was a little nervous about it. None of the other customers at the counter paid the slightest attention to him, though.

He arrived at 223 River Road a few minutes after one. The Quincy home was in the far north section of town, in the most exclusive beach area. It was a year-round beach home of two stories, perched at the edge of the river bluff over a stretch of spotless sand beach.

Parking a few doors away, he approached the house on foot. It was set well back from the road, as were all homes along here, and was separated from the places either side of it by a good hundred feet. A double garage with open doors contained a Ford station wagon. Presumably the vacant stall next to it ordinarily housed the red Chrysler convertible Velda had been driving on the sole occasion Horton had seen her.

Just before he left her, Helen had told him that the only servant was a cleaning woman who came twice a week, on Wednesdays and Saturdays. Nevertheless he took the precaution of ringing the doorbell.

When no one answered, he opened the door with the key Helen had given him and stepped inside. He found himself in a small entry hall. To his left an archway led into a living room. To his right a similar archway led into a dining room. Straight ahead was the stairway to the second floor. Beyond the stairway, at the end of the hall, was the open door to the kitchen.

As he paused to listen for some sound indicating that someone might be home after all, the distinct click of the back door closing came from the kitchen. Quickly but quietly, he reopened the front door, stepped outside, and closed it again.

Had the sound been made by someone entering or someone leaving, he wondered? If the latter, whoever it was must have heard his ring, and it seemed peculiar that it hadn't been answered. If it had been someone leaving, he should soon know. As there was nothing behind the house but the beach and the river, the person should appear around the corner at any moment.

Several seconds passed without anyone appearing. Then he was surprised to hear a car engine start from the direction of the river. The sound of the car driving away to the south came to him.

Stepping off the porch, he rounded the house to the edge of the bluff. On the smooth strip of sand beach twenty-five feet below were the distinct marks of tire treads. The tracks led south for the distance of about half a city block, then turned left onto a narrow road which ended at the beach.

Puzzled, he returned to the front door and pushed the doorbell again. Inside he heard musical chimes, but no one answered. He keyed open the door and entered for a second time. A cautious check of the whole downstairs disclosed no one there.

It must have been either the cleaning woman coming by for some forgotten item, or a friend of Velda's who had access to the house, he decided. But why had whoever it was gone to the trouble of driving around onto the beach? There was a railed stairway leading from the top of the bluff to the beach, but it would have been much more convenient for the mysterious visitor to come by the front way and park in the drive. And why hadn't the doorbell been answered?

A possible solution was that the visitor had no more authority to be there than he had.

Shrugging it off, he mounted the stairs and looked into each of the four rooms on the second floor. This floor was as deserted as the first.

Apparently, Honest John Quincy and his wife had maintained separate bedrooms, for one of the rooms was distinctly masculine and another was daintily feminine. The lack of any personal items in the remaining two tabbed them as guest rooms.

Horton opened the top dresser drawer in the masculine bedroom. The pistol was just where Helen had said it would be: beneath a pile of handkerchiefs.

It was a forty-five Colt automatic with hard-rubber grips. He ejected the clip, drew back the slide until it locked open to make sure no shell was in the chamber, then sniffed at the muzzle. He thought he could detect the faint smell of cordite, but it was too slight to be certain. Carrying the gun to the window, he inserted his little finger into the ejection slot so that the nail would act as a reflector, and peered down the barrel.

The gun had not been cleaned since it was last fired. How long that was, there was no way to determine.

Returning to the dresser, he picked up the clip and thumbed out the cartridges one at a time. There were only six, instead of a full load of seven. He reloaded the clip, snapped the slide forward, and shoved the clip back into the butt of the gun.

If he could locate something in the house soft enough to fire the gun into without distorting the slug, he preferred to make his test fire right there, so that he wouldn't have to make a return trip to plant the gun back where he had found it. A pillow to muffle the shot and a bucket of sand to catch the slug would serve fine, he decided. There was plenty of sand on the beach, probably some extra pillows which wouldn't be missed immediately in one of the closets, so the only problem was the bucket.

Carrying the gun downstairs, he located a mop bucket in a cabinet under the kitchen sink.

At the back door he paused with his hand on the knob. Through the glass pane in the top of the door he could see a whole party of people in bathing suits filing toward the river from the rear of the house next door. Though the house was a hundred feet away, he would be in full view of the party if he went down to the beach. And a stranger immaculately dressed in a sport coat, slacks and a snap-brim hat could hardly fail to excite curiosity when he began to collect sand in a bucket.

Horton reluctantly came to the conclusion that he had no choice but to take the gun away with him and return it later. Putting the bucket back where he had found it, he thrust the gun in his hip pocket and let himself out the front door.

He had to drive a mile back in the direction of downtown before he found a dime store. He spent two dollars of his dwindling supply of cash for a scrub bucket and a cheap pillow. Then he drove north again, clear beyond the edge of town, until he found a side road leading down to a strip of deserted beach.

The beach wasn't sand here, which was probably why it was deserted. It was a cindery type of dirt, too poor to grow anything but a few sparse weeds. However, it was loose enough soil so that he had no difficulty scooping the bucket full of it.

Glancing both ways along the beach, he saw no one. He laid the pillow on top of the bucket, threw a shell into the chamber of the automatic and pressed the muzzle deeply into the pillow. After one more quick look around, he fired.

The sound of the shot was only a muffled pop. Tossing the pillow aside, he dumped out the dirt and probed in the pile for the slug. When he unearthed it, he examined it carefully. It was a perfect specimen, not in the least misshapen.

Horton dropped it in his pocket along with the ejected brass cartridge case. Then he cleared the gun's chamber of the shell which had automatically replaced the ejected one when he fired, thumbed it back into the clip and shoved the clip back into the gun.

He left the pillow and the bucket lying on the beach. The gun he locked in the glove compartment of the car.

It was past two-thirty when he again drove by Velda's home. This time the red convertible was parked in the garage next to the station wagon, which meant she was now home.

Horton was a little surprised. Although the colonel had only guaranteed to keep her busy until two-thirty, it wasn't like him to let such a beautiful young woman escape him without a struggle after so short a time. Then, as he drove slowly past the house, he spotted the colonel's erect, portly figure standing in a front-room window. He had a glass in his hand.

Apparently, despite his sixty years, Velda had found him charming enough to bring home with her.

There was nothing further Horton could do until he could get in touch with the colonel. From a drugstore phone booth he dialed the Hotel Lawford and asked for Belle's room. Several rings sounded before she answered.

When she recognized his voice, she said, "You just barely caught me. The phone was ringing as I came in."

"I was afraid you might still be out," he said. "I saw you leaving."

"And I saw you. Very attractive redhead. What does she use?"

"Use?" he asked.

"To get that natural-looking hair color. Her skin practically screams that she's really a dishwater blonde, you know."

Horton said, "Don't be such a cat."

"She's the girl on the desk, isn't she? I might have known. She'd be the first woman you spoke to after you got in town. When you registered. What does she think of you after this morning's news write-up? Have you seen it?"

"No."

"She must have. It describes your past in colorful detail."

"She already knew about that," Horton told her.

"Oh?" Belle said on a rising note. "It's gotten to the point of confessing your sins to each other, has it? Doesn't she have any moral objection to your way of life?"

"Well, she wants me to reform."

"How touching. Are you going to?"

"I've been thinking about it," Horton said.

There was a moment of silence. Then Belle said in a different tone, "You mean it, don't you? You really like this girl."

"Yes, I do," he admitted.

"Enough to marry her?"

"I don't know. I can't even think about that until I've cleared myself of this mess."

After another short silence, Belle said, "Which means you have thought about it. I didn't realize, Jim. I was just being bitchy about her as a sort of a gag. I'm sorry. Her hair is really a natural red."

"For God's sake, don't play the understanding woman with me," he said in exasperation. "I feel enough like a heel now."

"I'm sorry," she said again. "How do you want me to act?"

"Like yourself. The way we've always been."

"Good friends, you mean? All right, Jim. We're good friends. What were you calling about?"

"I want to get in touch with the colonel. At the moment he's with Velda at her house. There's no telling how long he'll be there, but I suppose he'll phone you when he finally tears himself away, won't he?"

"If he has the strength. Isn't the woman supposed to be a nympho?" Her tone was very gay and brittle.

He said sourly, "That's the gossip."

"Poor Colonel Bob. At his age she may be fatal. What shall I tell him if he calls?"

"Arrange a meeting for this evening. I'll call you back about six to find out when and where. He should phone by then, shouldn't he?"

"Probably. Did you find what you were looking for?"

"Yeah. But I can't tell you about it over the phone. That's what I want to see the colonel about."

"I'll tell him," she said. "I'll expect your call back at six, then."

CHAPTER XX

The rest of the afternoon Horton idled away the time by taking a drive along the river. At five-thirty he stopped for dinner at a roadhouse a few miles north of town. Here he could hardly eat in his hat without exciting attention, so he removed it. For the first time since his description had been broadcast, he was exposing his close-cropped, sandy hair.

Neither his waiter nor any of the other diners exhibited any undue interest in his appearance.

It was six by the time he finished eating. He phoned Belle from the roadhouse.

"Colonel Bob phoned not ten minutes ago," she said. "From a bar on the north side. He said he'd wait for you there."

"What bar?"

"A place called Henry's Grill. 4220 North Reardon. He says it's a very quiet place."

"Okay," Horton said. "Thanks."

"Will I see you again?" Belle inquired in a suddenly diffident tone.

"Of course. What do you mean?"

"Well, I want to tell you good-by and good luck in person. Not just end it over the phone."

"Please, Belle," he said in a pained voice. "Why do you keep acting as though I've jilted you?"

"I'm sorry I upset you," she said. "I'm not trying to be dramatic. I just want to make sure I'll see you once more."

"Of course you will," he said a little testily.

"All right, Jim," she said, sounding a little lost. "I didn't mean to make you angry."

She hung up, and he stood for a moment with the phone still in his hand, blaming himself for snapping at her. It was a defense against having to admit his own feeling of guilt, he thought. He told himself he owed Belle nothing, that he'd never committed himself to anything but a casual affair, and that he shouldn't feel any guilt.

Nevertheless, when he finally hung the phone up, he still couldn't shake the feeling.

Henry's Grill was as average-looking a neighborhood tavern as the Hurricane Bar had been. At this time of evening, after the cocktail hour and before people started out after dinner, the place was almost deserted. The colonel stood at the bar alone, talking to a bartender as bald as he was.

As Horton entered the place, the bartender was saying, "You must have it wrong, mister. Doesn't make sense, the way you put it."

Colonel Bob was wearing a deliberate expression of stupidity. Puckering his brow in thought, he said, "I'm sure that's the way this fellow who showed it to me put it. Let's see now. I'll bet you a quarter that if you give me a half-dollar, I'll give you a dollar bill. Isn't that what I said before?"

"Yeah. But you come out a quarter loser that way. You must have it wrong." The bartender turned to Horton. "Yes, sir?"

After paying for his dinner, Horton was down to a dollar bill and some change. He ordered a beer. He gave no sign that he had ever before seen the colonel.

The bald barkeep drew a draft beer, set it before Horton and returned his attention to Colonel Bob.

"Let's try it out," he suggested. "Where's your dollar bill?"

Taking out his wallet, the colonel extracted a crisp one and handed it over for inspection. After examining it carefully, the barkeep handed it back.

"That's the dollar bill you'll give me for a half?" he inquired. "There's no trick about giving me some play money or something, huh?"

"I'm betting that I'll give you this specific dollar bill I have here in my hand," the colonel said, waving it. "Providing you first give me a half-dollar, of course." He laid a quarter on the bar. "Put up your money."

The bartender mentally checked his arithmetic once more, winked at Horton and reached in his pocket to lay a twenty-five-cent piece on top of the colonel's.

"Now give me your half-dollar," the colonel said.

The barkeep reached in his pocket again, produced a half-dollar and handed it over. "Okay," he said, holding out his palm. "Give me the dollar."

The colonel dropped both the dollar bill and the half into his pocket. "Pick up your money, sir," he said with a winning smile. "You win the bet."

The bartender stared at him for a moment, then looked down at the two quarters still lying on the bar. He picked them up and wrinkled his brow. Then his expression cleared. "Yeah. Say, that's pretty good. Worth two bits to learn it. Wait'll I work it on some of the wise apples who come in here."

Then he had a thought. "Hey, this would work just as good for real stakes. For instance, you could say, 'I'll bet you a dollar that if you give me a ten, I'll give you a twenty.' You'd make nine bucks instead of a lousy quarter."

Colonel Bob shook his head chidingly. "Fight a war of containment," he advised.

"Huh?"

"It's an established military principle that when the enemy is capable of massive retaliation, you commit only enough troops to harass him, unless you're prepared to withstand attack by his big guns."

The bartender said, "You're over my head, mister."

"I'll reduce it to a bartender-customer relationship. If you take a customer for a quarter, he'll laugh it off as a joke. Clip him for nine dollars, and he'll never come in again. You'd lost all your business."

After thinking this over, the barkeep gave a reluctant nod. "Guess you're right at that." Then he brightened. "I'm sure going to take a lot of these wise apples for two bits apiece, though."

The colonel turned to Horton. Addressing him in the polite tone of a stranger, he said, "Will you have a drink on my profits, sir?"

Horton indicated that he would have another beer. The colonel ordered scotch on the rocks.

When the drinks had been served, the colonel asked the bartender what he had to eat.

"Just short order stuff," the man said. "Sandwiches, chile, tripe."

Colonel Bob said, "I had a heavy lunch. All I want is a snack." He ordered a hot roast-beef sandwich.

When the bartender had disappeared into the kitchen, the colonel looked inquiringly at Horton. Horton produced the forty-five slug and dropped it into his hand.

"From the gun I found at Velda's place," he said. "Will you have your pals over at Ballistics run a comparison against the murder bullet?"

Colonel Bob examined the slug doubtfully. "How do I explain where I got it?"

"You had an anonymous phone call from someone who knew you were writing up the case for Fact Crime Magazine. The voice told you where to find it—a dime locker at the railroad station, for instance. You can make up some likely place. The caller told you to have it checked against the bullet that killed Quincy. Said he'd phone back tomorrow to find out if they matched. If they did, he'd tell you where to find the gun."

The colonel nodded. "Think they'll swallow that. Sounds logical enough." He dropped the slug into his pocket.

"If it does match, you can give me time enough to get the gun back into Velda's house, then tell the cops your anonymous informer tipped you to where it is. If the gun's registered to Quincy, that ought to take me off the hook altogether."

"You took the gun away with you?" the colonel asked. "Thought you were going to test it right there."

"Circumstances prevented it. How'd you make out with the lady?"

Colonel Bob looked offended. "No gentleman discusses such things," he said a trifle coldly. "No gentleman would ask."

"You've got a guilty conscience," Horton told him. "I mean, did you have any trouble convincing her you were a writer?"

"Oh," the colonel said, a little abashed. "Of course not. Matter of fact, we spent a good deal of time discussing the case."

"You did? Learn anything from her?"

"Nothing important. Naturally I couldn't bring up the rumor that Quincy was on the verge of divorcing her. It did come out that she knew about the gun her husband owned, though. Claims he couldn't find it?"

"What? What's she mean?"

"She was describing the evening the threatening note showed up. She found it in the mailbox, she said, and took it in to her husband. His first reaction was to go looking for his gun. It wasn't where he always kept it."

"He must not have looked very hard," Horton said. "Or else it never happened. What do you make of her story?"

The colonel shrugged. "Sounded like the truth. I didn't inquire about the gun. Couldn't, without making her wonder how I knew Quincy had owned one. She volunteered the information without prodding. It came out quite naturally, while she was describing her husband's reaction to the threat."

"Hmm," Horton said. "Suggests a guilty conscience, doesn't it?"

"How?" the colonel inquired, raising one eyebrow.

"She seems to have gone out of her way to let you know the gun disappeared before the murder. Yet it was still in its usual place today. Why would she mention it, unless she was trying to plant the idea that she couldn't have used it on her husband?"

"Why would she mention it even if she did kill him? Why not let sleeping dogs lie?"

"That's what I meant about a guilty conscience," Horton said. "She must have brought it up because it's on her mind. Nobody but the killer would know that Quincy's gun had any bearing on the case."

"One other possible explanation," the colonel said.

"What?"

"She may simply have been telling the truth."

The bartender interrupted their conversation then by coming from the kitchen with the colonel's hot roast-beef sandwich.

CHAPTER XXI

"Where you want it?" the barkeep asked the colonel.

Colonel Bob nodded toward a booth. "Care to join me and have another beer, sir?" he asked Horton.

Horton said, "I'll have a cup of coffee with you."

"Make that two," the colonel told the bartender.

They seated themselves and the bartender returned to the kitchen for the coffee. The colonel looked after him thoughtfully.

"Seems to me he was looking you over rather closely," he said.

Horton glanced at him in surprise. "I didn't notice it."

When the barkeep returned with the coffee, Horton surreptitiously watched him. The man didn't seem to be paying him any more attention than he did the colonel.

Setting the coffee and two cream containers before them, the bartender asked, "Anything else, gentlemen?"

Both shook their heads. The bartender returned to the kitchen. They could hear him begin to rattle dishes back there.

"Probably my overactive imagination," the colonel said.

"I've got one too," Horton told him. "I start sweating every time somebody gives me a second glance. But I didn't notice this fellow eyeing me particularly."

The colonel started to eat his sandwich. After a moment Horton said, "Still have your friend Tyrell on the string?"

The colonel affixed him with his invisible monocle. "How'd you learn his name? Belle been talking?"

Grinning, Horton shook his head. "I eavesdropped last Friday evening when Belle was dining with him. Sidetracking you this way isn't going to make you lose out with him, is it?"

Colonel Bob smiled. "It's only whet his appetite. The delay's killing him. He's afraid I may change my mind and not let him in on the deal."

Conversation lapsed then, as the colonel disposed of his sandwich and Horton sipped his coffee. When he finished the sandwich, the colonel produced two cigars and offered one to Horton.

Horton shook his head. The colonel returned one to his pocket, started to strip cellophane from the other, then stopped the movement and slowly returned it to his pocket too. With suddenly narrowed eyes, he glanced over his shoulder at the kitchen door.

"Hasn't been any sound from there in some time," he said softly. "There's a phone on the wall back there, too. Noticed it through the open door when we were at the bar."

Instantly Horton became alert. He too looked toward the kitchen door. He strained his ears against a silence which suddenly seemed ominous.

Quietly the colonel slipped from the booth and peered out the front window. Then he turned and made an urgent gesture toward an open door at the end of the bar through which stairs descending to the cellar could be seen.

"Cops," he said in a barely audible voice. "I'll stall them."

Without a sound, Horton moved toward the stairs, his eyes on the door to the kitchen. The bartender was not in sight.

The only spot from which he could be seen from the kitchen door was the end of the bar. He passed behind it on his hands and knees and scuttled through the basement doorway. He was halfway down the stairs when he heard the sound of the tavern's front door opening. Quietly, he descended the rest of the way and moved in under the stairs.

A deep voice said with surprise, "Why, hello, Major. What are you doing here?"

Apparently the colonel had slid back into the booth, for his voice came from that direction. "Lieutenant Grady. This is a happy chance. I was just going to phone you."

The voice of the bartender came from the kitchen doorway. "You men police officers?" he asked anxiously.

"Yeah," a fourth voice said. "Where is he?"

"He was sitting right there in the booth with this gentleman," the bartender said excitedly. "I recognized him from his description. Where'd he go, mister?"

"The man I was talking to?" the colonel asked. "Why he walked out some time ago. What's this all about?"

Grady's deep voice said, "Who was he, Major?"

Horton could almost see the colonel's shrug. "Just a man I fell into conversation with at the bar, Lieutenant. He didn't offer his name. What's it all about?"

"This guy phoned in that Quincy's killer was here. We got half the force surrounding this place."

"You mean that Horton fellow?" the colonel inquired. "Oh, come now, Lieutenant. Wouldn't that be quite a coincidence?"

"What?"

"I mean my casually running into him at a bar. When I'm doing research on the very murder he's accused of. Things like that just don't happen."

"You mean it wasn't him?"

There was a thoughtful silence on the colonel's part. "Now that I think of it, he did answer the newspaper description pretty well," he finally admitted. "Except for his hair. Papers described Horton as wearing a crew cut."

"He had a hat on," the bartender said. "You couldn't see his hair. It was him all right. Fitted his description to a tee."

"Yeah?" Grady said. "Well, we'll take a look around. You check the washrooms, Cassidy. I'll take a look in the basement."

Footsteps began to move toward the cellar door. Horton took a quick glance around. The only illumination in the basement came from a couple of narrow, dirt-encrusted windows at street level. It was just enough to show two doors. One, padlocked shut, was probably to a liquor storeroom. The other had a heavy refrigerator-door handle and was obviously to the beer-cooler.

The stairway was the only way out of the basement.

Grady's foot was on the top step when the colonel's voice said, "You're wasting time, Lieutenant. I saw him walk out the front door. If it was your man, you'd better start a search of the neighborhood before he gets clear away."

There was a heart-stopping pause, then the lieutenant's foot withdrew and he walked back into the upstairs room. "Cassidy!" he called.

"Yes, sir?"

"Forget the washrooms. Tell the boys outside to spread out through the area. Have them check every tavern and store that's open. And keep a lookout for him on the street. Hey, bartender. What was he wearing again?"

"A light gray plaid sport jacket, gray slacks, brown shoes and a brown hat. White shirt and a red-and-blue plaid tie. I looked him over real good and memorized it."

"Got it," Cassidy's voice said. "Okay, Lieutenant. I'll put the boys on it."

The sound of the front door opening and closing again came to Horton.

Grady said, "You mentioned you were going to phone me, Major. What about?"

"I got a funny telephone call," the colonel said. "Tell you about it outside. Don't want to keep you from your men. How much do I owe you, bartender?"

"Forty for the sandwich. Twenty for your coffee and that other guy's coffee. Sixty cents."

There was a short silence, then the ding of the cash register and the sound of change being slapped on the bar. Two sets of footsteps moved toward the door.

As the door opened, the colonel's voice said, "This was an anonymous call, Lieutenant. Fellow phoned me at the Rafferty House. Said he'd heard I was writing up the Quincy case for Fact Crime Mag—"

The rest was cut off by the door closing behind them.

Upstairs there was the sound of the bartender drawing himself a glass of beer. He muttered something to himself which Horton couldn't catch.

Horton glanced around the basement again. Then, stepping soundlessly on the balls of his feet, he made a circuit of it. The two windows were too narrow to get through, and, anyway, they were nailed shut. They couldn't possibly be opened without the sound being heard upstairs.

Even if it had been possible to sneak past the bartender, there was no point in trying to leave the basement while police were still in the area. Horton quietly upended a beer case behind the furnace and sat on it. Here he would be out of sight if the bartender had to come downstairs to tap a new keg, or to get bottles from the liquor storeroom.

He settled down to wait until it was safe to make a break.

CHAPTER XXII

Horton decided to give the police two hours to convince themselves he had escaped from the neighborhood. It was now seven P.M. He would make his break at nine.

At ten minutes after seven he heard the first evening customer arrive. When he heard him exchange greetings with the bartender, Horton moved over beneath the stairs to listen for a few moments.

First the sound of a beer being drawn came to him, then the clink of the glass being set on the bar. The cash register dinged.

"Had a little excitement here a few minutes ago," the bartender said. "Guy answering the description of Quincy's killer dropped in and had a couple of beers as big as you please. I phoned the cops from the kitchen, and they came swarming all over the place. He took off, though, before they got here."

"I'll be darned," the customer said.

Another customer came in, and after serving his drink, the bartender repeated the story. Horton went back to his seat behind the furnace.

During the next hour and a half the barroom gradually filled up. It seemed to be strictly a men's bar, for Horton couldn't detect a single feminine voice from above.

Several times he moved back beneath the stairs to listen to the conversation. The bartender was telling each new arrival about Quincy's killer dropping in, and how he recognized him and phoned the police. Eventually, when everyone in the place had heard the incident several times, he recalled the con game the colonel had worked on him.

"Hey," Horton heard him say. "I got a good one to show you. I'll bet you a quarter that if you give me a half, I'll give you a dollar bill."

Unfortunately the bartender didn't possess the colonel's skill at getting people to make bets with him. None of the customers seemed willing to bite. Horton listened for some minutes as the man explained the bet over and over, without getting any takers. Apparently no one was able to figure out the catch, but their reluctance suggested that they knew there must be a catch somewhere, and none of them wanted to be shown up as suckers.

"The devil with all of you," the bartender finally said in a disgusted tone. "Too cheap to risk two bits on a sure thing." Then he called, "Hey, Charlie. Watch the bar for me a minute, will you? I got to tap one."

He moved to the basement door and was clattering down the stairs before Horton could start back for his refuge behind the furnace. It happened so quickly, Horton could do nothing but flatten himself against the wall beneath the stairs and hope he wouldn't be seen.

He was safe enough from observation while the man was on the way to the cooler, for when he turned toward it at the bottom of the stairs, his back was to Horton. But when he came out of the cooler to return upstairs, Horton would be right in front of him.

Horton waited until he entered the cooler and bent over the empty barrel with his back to the door. Then, on tiptoe, he headed toward the furnace. He had to pass the cooler's open door to get there.

He thought he was going to make it. He was almost past the door when the bartender completed drawing the tap hose from the empty and started to roll the barrel out of the way. The movement turned him sidewise enough to glimpse Horton's figure from the corner of his eye.

With a startled exclamation he came erect and stared at Horton. Horton came to a halt.

"You!" the bartender said.

There was only one thing to do, and Horton did it. Stepping into the cooler, he brought around a fast right hook with all the power of his shoulder behind it. It caught the man squarely on the point of the jaw. His eyes crossed and he pitched forward into Horton's arms.

Backing out of the cooler, Horton gently lowered the unconscious man to the floor. He pushed shut the cooler door and moved to the stairs. Taking a deep breath, he started up.

Every seat at the bar was filled, and most of the booths were occupied. As Horton stepped from the cellar door, a man at the end of the bar glanced at him casually, then examined him more sharply.

When Horton gave him a sunny smile and moved on past, the man relaxed, nodded and returned his attention to his drink. No one else seemed to notice Horton.

Without hurry he opened the door and stepped outside. The rented Ford was parked a quarter block up the street. Momentarily, he expected either the hue and cry of pursuit from the barroom, or for police to descend on him from concealment. Neither happened, however.

He pulled away from the curb slowly, drove at moderate speed to the first intersection, and turned right. After driving six blocks at the same speed without encountering a police barricade, he began to relax. He turned south and drove toward the center of town. At the first chain drugstore he spotted in the downtown area, he stopped to make a phone call.

Belle didn't answer her phone. He dropped another dime, called the Lawford again and asked for room 786.

Helen was in.

When she recognized his voice, she said in a tone of relief, "I've been so worried, Jim. How did you make out at Velda's?"

Before answering, he took his usual precaution of calling to the switchboard operator. When she failed to respond, he said, "Fine. But I'm in a bit of a jam now. I was recognized by somebody."

"Oh, goodness," she said. "What happened?"

"Tell you when I see you. The point is, they have the description of the clothes I'm wearing now. Probably there's a bulletin out to every cop in town. I have to hole up somewhere fast."

"You know you're welcome here," she said.

"Yeah. I also know I'd be risking your neck. Hiding out a wanted man is a criminal offense."

"Why do you even mention that?" she asked softly. "Don't you know I'd do anything for you?"

"Would you, Helen?"

"Of course. Besides, I know you're innocent."

"Maybe everybody will know it by tomorrow," he said. "How can I get up there?"

"The same way as before. Use the side entrance and come to the freight elevator. I'll bring it down to the lower hall and hold it there until you arrive. How soon will you be?"

"Fifteen minutes," he told her.

It took him only ten minutes to drive to the hotel. He parked on the street alongside it and carefully looked up and down before getting out of the car. A few pedestrians were on the street, but he saw no police uniforms.

Locking the car, he quickly moved to the side entrance and stepped into the entryway. Instead of going straight ahead into the lobby, he took the hall leading off the entryway to the right. This led to the rear hall where the freight elevator was.

At the corner where the two hallways joined, he paused and drew back out of sight while a waiter with a tray of food on his shoulder crossed the hall from the kitchen into the dining room. As soon as the swinging doors into the dining room closed after the waiter, he hurried past to the freight elevator.

It was on the ground floor and Helen was waiting in the car as she had promised. The instant he stepped inside, the door closed and they began to rise.

Neither said anything. At the seventh floor Helen checked the hallway before motioning him out of the car. She checked again at both turns of the corridor on the way to her room. They encountered no one.

Safely inside the room, both of them heaved sighs of relief. Horton sailed his hat onto the bed, shrugged out of his sport coat and loosened his tie.

"Sure good to be home," he said.

"It's good to have you," Helen said with a smile.

She moved against him and slid her arms about his neck. After he had kissed her, she drew back to look up into his face.

"It's been awful," she said. "All day I've been imagining you in the hands of the police. Or worse, in the hands of Manzetti. Why can't you just stay here now until this is all over?"

"It's a pleasant thought," Horton said dryly. "But I doubt that it'd ever be over if I just sat and waited for it to end. I'll have to go out again tomorrow."

"Why?" she asked.

"I had to take the gun away from Velda's. It's in the glove compartment of a rented car I have downstairs. A friend of mine's having a test slug from it checked against the murder bullet. If they match, I'll have to plant the gun back at Velda's again."

"And then it will be over?" she asked.

"It ought to convince the police I didn't kill your stepfather. It'll be up to Velda to explain the gun."

She moved out of his arms with a thoughtful little frown on her face. "What if you got caught before you could put it back? With the murder gun in your possession?"

"We haven't established it as the murder gun yet," he said. "We're just hoping."

"But suppose it really is, and you got caught with it?"

"That would cook me good," he said. "Let's not think about it. How about mixing up a couple of drinks?"

CHAPTER XXIII

Helen had the next morning off in order to attend her step-father's funeral at ten. As Velda would presumably attend it too, this would be a good opportunity for Horton to replace the forty-five automatic.

They had breakfast in Helen's room again, then Helen left for the funeral parlor at nine-thirty. Horton rang Belle's room, found her in and said he would be right over.

This time Belle was fully dressed when he got there. She made no mention of his presence at the hotel again, and its obvious implication that he had spent the night with Helen. Her manner was subdued and she seemed to be on guard against saying anything to offend Horton. He got the impression that she was determined not to show any further jealousy, nor to give him any other excuse to accuse her of dramatics.

He should have felt relieved, but her stoic attitude only increased his feeling of guilt about the whole matter.

A little brusquely he asked permission to use her phone, and called the Rafferty House. When he got hold of the colonel, he asked if there had been a report from Lieutenant Grady on the bullet comparison as yet. The colonel said he hadn't heard from Grady, but would phone police headquarters immediately and then call Horton back.

He phoned back ten minutes later.

"Jackpot," he told Horton. "It was the murder gun, all right. I promised to let Grady know the minute my anonymous informer called to tell me where the gun could be found."

"Better wait till I give you the go-ahead," Horton said. "I plan to put it back while Velda's at the funeral this morning. But hold off till you hear from me, in case there's a slip-up."

"Right-o," the colonel said, slipping into one of his rare Briticisms.

When he hung up, Belle said, "Is there anything I can do, Jim?"

"You could act as lookout on the way to the car," Horton said. "I'd hate to be spotted by someone on the way out of the hotel, now that it's so close to over."

"All right," Belle agreed.

She checked the hallway to make sure it was empty, then crossed it and pushed the freight elevator button. Horton waited in her room with the door cracked open until the elevator door slid open and he saw that the car was unoccupied. Then he quickly crossed the hall and entered the elevator behind her.

Horton had observed Helen's manipulation of the controls enough to know how to work them. The contraption had bastard controls. Originally designed to be run by an operator, it had been rewired so that it could be called to any floor by pressing a call button. The original lever control hadn't been replaced by a panel of buttons, however, so that once inside the car it had to be operated in the old-fashioned way. Horton pushed down on the lever, watched the painted floor numbers as they flashed by, and slowly began to raise the lever again as they passed the second floor. He brought the car to a jerky stop a foot too high, lowered it to the proper level in two jolting drops of six inches each, and the doors slid open.

He stayed in the car until Belle gave him the all-clear, then followed her rapid pace past the kitchen to the turn in the hall and on into the side entryway. Before stepping outdoors, he checked the street through the glass. There were no police uniforms in sight and no one was near the parked Ford.

"I can make it from here," he said. "Thanks, Belle."

"Want me to go with you?" she asked. "I have nothing else to do."

He looked at her contemplatively. "If I get picked up, you'd be in a jam."

"Why?" she inquired. "I met you at a bar, and had no idea you were wanted by the police. I've talked my way out of worse spots."

Horton shrugged. "Come along, if you want."

He gave another quick glance at the street, then took her elbow and led her to the car.

It was past ten thirty when he parked a half block away from 223 River Road. Horton figured the funeral would keep Velda away until at least noon, so he was in no particular hurry. Unlocking the glove compartment, he lifted out the automatic and thrust it into his belt under his sport jacket.

"You'd better wait in the car," he told Belle.

Horton came to an abrupt halt when he reached the walk leading up to the house. Through the open doors of the garage he could see both the Chrysler convertible and the Ford station wagon. Doing an about-face, he went back to the car.

"What's the matter?" Belle asked.

Climbing behind the wheel, Horton pushed up his hat to give the back of his head a puzzled scratch. "Both cars are in the garage."

Belle stared at him for a moment, then shook her head wonderingly. "And I called you a genius."

He glanced at her. "What's that supposed to mean?"

"Widows don't drive themselves to their husbands' funerals alone, mastermind. They ride in one of the mourners' cars. Someone picked her up and took her to the funeral."

"Oh," Horton said a little blankly. He got out of the car again, gave Belle a shamefaced look, and walked up the street a second time.

As on his previous visit, he took the precaution of ringing the doorbell. When there was no answer, he unlocked the door and started to push it open.

A burglar chain stopped its movement after it opened only a few inches.

Clicking the door shut again, he stood considering what this meant. After a moment he decided that probably all it meant was that Velda had left by the rear door, and therefore quite naturally had not released the chain on the front. A glance at the driveway running alongside the house convinced him the chain had no more serious implications. He saw that if the car calling for her had pulled clear back to the garage to turn around, it would be closer to the rear door than to the front. It would be logical for Velda to have gone out that way.

Circling the house, he tried the rear door and found it locked. All the first-floor windows were locked too. He made another circle of the house, checking the basement windows and door, with equal lack of success.

He returned to the car again and leaned in the front window.

"Finally finished?" Belle asked. "I was beginning to worry. You've been gone twenty minutes."

"I'm not even started," he told her. "She left a chain on the front door. Got a rubber band?"

She raised her eyebrows, then opened her purse and searched through it. Horton waited patiently as she laid out a multitude of items on the seat next to her. As one after another there appeared a cigarette case, a lighter, a compact, lipstick, comb, handkerchief, wallet, change purse, address book, pen, pencil and, finally, a small packet of snapshots, it struck him that watching a woman empty her purse was similar to watching a certain circus act: the one in which an unending number of dwarf clowns tumbled from the interior of a miniature truck.

Belle slipped a rubber band from around the packet of snapshots and handed it to him.

"What's it for?" she asked.

"An old burglar's stunt my mother once taught me," he said. "I shouldn't be long now."

Returning to the house again, he glanced at the homes on either side, then keyed open the door a second time. Inserting his left hand in the crack, he slipped one end of the rubber band over the small knob of the chain catch, doubled it around the knob until there was only a short piece of the rubber band left, and stretched it to hook over the far end of the slotted bar in which the chain catch rode.

Then he withdrew his hand and pulled the door nearly shut.

He could hear the chain catch slide along its slot as the tension of the rubber band drew it away from the edge of the door. His hope was that when the catch reached the insertion hole at the end of the slot, the rubber band would become loose enough to slip from the end of the bar. If it didn't, the catch couldn't fall free, he would have to release a little of the rubber band's tension by unwinding one of its turns around the knob, and try over.

He had guessed the proper tension the first time. The chain rattled as the catch tumbled from the insertion hole.

Horton pushed open the door and went in.

Glancing at his watch, he saw that it was now eleven o'clock. His trying of windows and doors, his two trips back to the car and the rubber-band trick had consumed nearly a half hour. He decided he had better get his business completed in a hurry and get out of the place.

Upstairs he carefully wiped the automatic free of fingerprints and concealed it under the handkerchiefs in the dead man's top dresser drawer. After wiping the knobs of the drawer, he heaved a sigh of relief.

There was an extension phone on a table next to the bed. Horton saw no point in delaying his call to Colonel Bob until he could reach a drugstore. Lifting the phone, he dialed the Rafferty House.

When he got the colonel on the phone, he said, "You can call your friend, Grady, now. It's all set."

"Fine," the colonel said with satisfaction. "Where are you?"

"At Velda's house. I'm just leaving. I'll stay out of sight for the rest of the day, and call you about six to find out what the police did about the gun. As soon as they arrest Velda, I'll turn myself in."

"Fine," the colonel said again. "I'll expect to hear from you at six then."

Horton wiped his prints from the phone and started toward the bed-room door. In the doorway he came to a sudden halt. Downstairs he heard the sound of the back door opening.

Then he heard Velda's soft drawl saying, "Thanks very much, Mrs. Corby. No, I'll be all right, really. I think I prefer to be alone."

A woman's voice said something Horton didn't catch, and the door clicked shut. A moment later there was the sound of a car leaving the driveway. Velda's footsteps moved to the front of the house. He heard the front door open, and for a moment had the wild hope that she was immediately going out again.

But apparently she had only checked the mailbox. When the front door closed again, he heard her shuffling through envelopes in the lower hall. Tiptoeing to the top of the stairs, he peeked over the railing in time to see her toss several unopened letters onto a small table in the hall.

He retreated back into Quincy's bedroom as she started up the stairs. Flattening himself against the wall alongside the door, he waited for her to go past to her own room. Once she entered that, he might be able to slip out and down the stairs without being heard.

She didn't go to her own room. She turned into her deceased husband's, walked right past Horton without seeing him and over to the dresser. Opening the top dresser drawer, she probed beneath the handkerchiefs and brought out the automatic Horton had just replaced there. She stared down at it in astonishment.

"It's back!" she said aloud in an amazed tone.

Then she saw Horton's reflection in the mirror over the dresser.

Whirling with the speed of a cat, she pointed the gun at him. There was a long moment of silence.

Then she said in a wondering voice, "Well, well. The pleasant young man who murdered my husband. Raise you hands, please."

CHAPTER XXIV

Instead of complying with the order, Horton merely stood with his hands at his sides and looked her up and down with deliberation.

She wore a plain black dress which might have passed for conventional mourning attire on another woman. But even with its decorously high neck and wrist-length sleeves, it didn't suggest mourning on Velda. Skin tight, it only served to outline every one of her curves. Perched on her head was a tiny black hat with a veil pushed up to her forehead. The hat added an incongruously civilized touch to an otherwise pagan picture. With the gun in her hand, and with her graceful body in the sinuous crouch of a panther ready to spring, Velda looked like some wicked priestess from an H. Rider Haggard novel.

Slowly Horton walked toward her. The gun's safety clicked off. He halted three feet away.

"If you think I won't shoot, take one more step," she said quietly.

But her threatening attitude was oddly tempered by the look of appraisal on her face. Even holding him at gunpoint, she was unable to resist estimating him as a man.

Horton said calmly, "I'm kind of curious to see if you will," and took another step toward her.

Velda's nostrils flared and she squeezed the trigger.

Horton gave her a wolfish grin as the hammer clicked home, took a final step and jerked the gun from her hand.

"There has to be a shell in the chamber," he said. "Like this." He drew back the slide, let it slam forward again and pointed the gun at her. "Now it will work fine."

Velda drew in her breath and her eyes widened enormously. "What do you want?" she whispered.

Horton clicked on the safety, lowered the gun and contemplated her. "Nothing, really. I was just trying to get out of the house without you seeing me. Wasn't it rather a fast funeral?"

She stared at him, saw from his inquiring expression that he really expected an answer and said mechanically, "It was a cremation. They don't take long. What are you doing in my house?"

"Bringing your husband's gun back," he said, wagging it. "I meant to leave quietly and let the police find it, but now I think I'll wait till they arrive. You might try to get rid of it if I left you alone."

"It was you who took the gun?" she asked. "Why? What did you have against John?"

The question puzzled him. "What?"

"If you went to the trouble to steal his own gun to kill him with, you didn't kill him for the reason the papers said. You planned it to look like I did it. Why?"

Horton said, "Are you under the impression I came here and stole this gun *before* the murder?"

"Well, didn't you?"

He frowned at her. "I took it yesterday, made a test firing and had the bullet compared to the murder slug. When I was satisfied it was the murder gun, I brought it back for the police to find. What are you trying to pull?"

Her mouth rounded to a small circle. "You mean you didn't kill John?"

"Come off it," he said impatiently. "You think with your husband's gun tabbed as the murder weapon, you can get away with the innocent act? Nobody but you had access to it."

"I didn't. It was gone before the murder. John looked for it the night the threat arrived."

"Sure," he said cynically. "You'd already hidden it somewhere else. If you think you can wriggle out by getting the cops to believe I burglarized your house for a gun in order to kill your husband, think again. They bought the theory that I killed him to avoid arrest, but you'd never in a million years convince them it was premeditated murder by me. You have to have a motive to pull a premeditated kill. And I never saw your husband until a few minutes before he died. Is this gun registered with the police?"

After staring at him for a moment, she said huskily, "I don't know."

"You can bet it is," he said confidently. "The chairman of the Civic Crime Committee wouldn't be likely to own an unregistered gun. And with your motive, you're cooked. Everybody in the know has heard the rumor that Quincy was divorcing you."

Velda ran the pink tip of her tongue over her lips. In a low voice she said, "You really didn't kill him, did you? I believe you."

"You ought to," he said cynically. "Since you pulled the trigger yourself."

"I didn't," she insisted. "It's another frame-up. Everybody was framed for this. First Manzetti, then you, now me."

"Sure. But it fits you best. Why'd you tell the police you never left home Saturday, when you were at the used-car lot only a few minutes before your husband's murder?"

"I thought it would help you," she said in an earnest voice. "I figured you'd done me a favor by killing him, and I didn't wish you any harm. I didn't want to have to testify that I'd seen you there."

"Yeah," he said without belief.

"You've got to believe me." Tentatively she reached out to touch his shoulder. "I swear I didn't kill him. Until this morning it never even occurred to me he might have been killed with that gun. Until Helen accused me to my face."

"Helen?" he said, startled. "Helen Quincy?"

"Yes. At the funeral. I knew she hated me, but I never thought she'd say a thing like that. She was awful."

"What'd she say?"

"She said I might at least have had the grace to stay home from the funeral of the man I killed. I was so flabbergasted, all I could do was ask what she meant. She accused me of using John's own gun on him. She said that when the police checked it, they'd know the truth and I'd pay for what I'd done. That's why I came straight here when I got home. To make sure the gun was still missing. I was never so surprised in my life to find it there."

Momentarily Horton was nearly as flabbergasted as Velda claimed she had been to hear of Helen's outburst. Then understanding hit him when Velda said, "Even hysterics is no excuse for her to talk to me like that."

Even uncomplicated funerals are conducive to feminine hysterics. With Helen believing Velda had married her step-father only for his money, and now convinced that the woman murdered him, it was no wonder she had lost control when she saw Velda at the funeral. Under the stress of her emotions, it wouldn't have occurred to Helen that lashing out at Velda might give her warning to dispose of the gun.

"Look," he said in a tone of finality. "I don't care who killed your husband. I just know I didn't, and I'm not about to take the rap for it. The police are going to find this gun right where it was. If you can talk your way around the evidence, you have my blessing. But don't expect my help. I'm concerned solely with getting myself off the hook."

Gently but firmly, he pushed her aside from the dresser. Wiping the gun again, he replaced it in the top drawer. Then he took Velda's elbow and steered her to the door.

"Where are we going?" she asked, trying to hold back.

"Downstairs to wait for the police."

She resisted, but she was no match for his strength. Relentlessly he forced her down the stairs and into the front room. When he finally released her arm, she rubbed the place he had gripped her and glared at him with indignation.

"Don't get any ideas about making a break for the stairs," he said. "Or for anywhere else. Just relax until the police arrive."

Tossing her head, she walked over to stare out one of the front-room windows. Watchfully, Horton followed, ready to grab her if she suddenly tried to run. Halting behind her, he glanced through the window over her shoulder.

Across the street a gray Oldsmobile sedan was parked with a man in the front seat and two in the back. As the house was set well back from the street, the car was too far away to make out the men's faces.

Horton smiled grimly. "Police stake-outs," he guessed. "Lieutenant Grady isn't taking any chances of your sneaking the evidence out of the house while he's getting a search warrant. It's not more than fifteen minutes since I phoned in. Pretty fast work."

Velda turned slowly and looked up into his face.

"Why do you want to do this to me?" she asked. "I told you I didn't kill him."

"Neither did I. And the gun will prove it."

"Don't you care that you'll get out of it only at the expense of another innocent person?"

Horton shrugged. "I'm not making up evidence to convict you. All I did was put the gun back where I found it. If you're being framed, I'm not the framer."

"Maybe together we could figure out who the real killer is," she urged. "It must have been one of Manzetti's men. He meant to frame me, then when you accidentally got the blame, he just didn't bother to go through with the original plan. All Manzetti would care about would be not to be suspected himself."

"It's possible," Horton admitted. "Maybe you can sell it to the police."

Her hands slid up to his shoulders. "If you'll let me hide the gun before they get here, we'll work on the solution together. I'd make it worth your while. In every way."

"How?"

"Financially, for one way. Could you use ten thousand dollars?"

"You'll inherit at least the widow's portion of over a million dollars if you aren't convicted," he said dryly. "Don't be so generous. What's another way?"

She tilted her head until her lips were just below his chin. "You seemed to like me the day we met. I remember how you kept looking at me. I felt the same way."

"Don't you always?" he asked with amusement.

"What?" she said with a frown.

Over her shoulder Horton saw one of the men get out of the car across the street and stare in their direction. Then he bent to say something to his two companions, and they started to get out of the car too.

Horton dropped his gaze to Velda's upturned face. "Too late," he said with mock regret. "They're starting to move in right now."

Firmly he removed her hands from his shoulders and moved to the center of the room. Velda gave him a stricken look and turned to peer out the window. Then she swiveled back and looked at him pleadingly.

"Please," she said. "They're coming up the walk. I won't have a chance if they find that gun. And I didn't do it. I'll pay you twenty thousand."

"I'm sorry," Horton said with a shake of his head. "Argue it out with the cops."

The door chimes sounded, and when she made no move to answer, Horton went to the door. Flipping off the lock, he swung the door wide.

Then, unsuccessfully, he tried to slam it closed again. Instead of police officers, Joey the Cut, Hippo and Russ stood outside. Joey caught the closing door with his shoulder at the same moment he snaked a forty-five pistol into sight. Stiff-arming Horton backward, he pushed into the entry hall and centered the gun between Horton's eyes. His two companions came in behind him. Russ pushed the door shut with a click of finality.

"Thanks for standing in the window, sucker," Joey said with a totally humorless grin. "We've been tailing Velda for two days in the hope you'd show, but we never would of suspected you was in the house if you hadn't been stupid enough to start loving her up right in the front-room window."

CHAPTER XXV

While Joey held Horton under his gun, Russ patted his pockets, legs and beneath his arms in a quick but expert shakedown.

"He's not carrying anything," he informed Joey.

Joey motioned toward the front room with his gun. When Horton obeyed the gesture, the three men trailed through the archway after him. Velda was still standing by the window, her hands clasped before her and her eyes hopelessly staring at the floor.

"You've got a reprieve, Velda," Horton said to her. "They aren't police officers. They're Tony Manzetti's men."

Velda's head jerked up and she stared at the three men. Her eyes widened at the gun in Joey Ault's hand.

"I don't understand," she said slowly.

In a cold voice Joey said to her, "Looks like Tony's first theory was right after all. You got Jimmy-boy here to rub your husband and set Tony up for the rap."

Velda looked from Joey to Horton without understanding.

"Manzetti had the idea that I killed your husband in conspiracy with you," Horton explained. "I talked him into a different theory, but now Joey here is convinced the first one was right. He thinks what he saw through the window was a love scene."

Velda raised her chin imperiously. "What do you men want?" she demanded.

Fat Hippo said, "Come off it, babe. You know what we want. To take Tony off the spot you tried to fix for him."

Horton said, "You gentlemen in the mood to listen before you go off half-cocked?"

Joey looked at him with hate. "I heard enough from you Sunday night, mister."

"You're wasting your time," Horton said. "I've got it set up so that both Manzetti and I are in the clear. Tony's Sunday-night plans are passé now. He doesn't need me dead any more."

Russ said, "Yeah? Not according to our orders."

Horton said patiently, "The police are on their way here right now with a search warrant. They'll find the gun that killed Quincy upstairs in a dresser drawer. It was Quincy's own gun. Nobody but Velda had access to it. It'll pin the rap squarely on her and let both Manzetti and me off the hook. If you're smart, you men will get out of here before the police arrive."

Joey merely continued to glare at Horton. Hippo regarded him with stolid indifference. Only Russ looked thoughtful.

"Maybe we better listen to this," he suggested to Joey.

"Listen hell," Joey told him coldly. "Tony said clean up the case by rigging a suicide. That's what we do." He turned to Velda. "You're gonna get lucky, sister. Tony don't care about your part in this. All he wants is a nice clean confession by your boy friend. A confession by suicide. You just sit tight, and you'll stay out of the chair for your part of it."

"What part?" Velda asked confusedly.

With mild impatience Joey said, "Don't play dumb with us, lady. Conspiracy to murder draws the same jolt as pulling the trigger. You let out a yap that we walked out of here with your boy friend, and we'll toss you to the wolves. You'll squat in the chair right next to him."

Velda suddenly looked hopeful. "You plan to take him away and arrange it so that there's no doubt that he killed my husband?"

"You got it, lady. And you're in no position to yell copper. You'd yell yourself right into the chair."

"I wouldn't say a word," Velda said with enthusiasm. "The murder gun's right upstairs. If you arranged it with that, it would be even added proof of his guilt."

"Hey!" Horton said. "A minute ago you were begging me to help you find the real killer."

"You should have accepted," she spat at him. She turned back to Joey. "Let me show you the gun. We'll have to hurry. The police may be here any minute."

Joey snapped orders to Russ and Hippo to cover Horton, waited until they drew guns and then gestured Velda toward the stairway. In the archway he paused to look back.

"Don't go to sleep this time," he growled at the two men.

Russ and Hippo showed no intention of it. They stood well back from Horton with their guns trained on him.

As Velda and Joey disappeared up the stairs, Horton said, "Tony's not going to like it if you unnecessarily complicate things. Joey just wants the pleasure of bumping me off because I conned him. If Tony was here, he'd tell you to leave it the way I've got it set up."

Neither man said anything.

"Don't let Joey steer you into risking a murder rap that's not necessary," Horton urged. "Why don't you phone Tony and explain the situation?"

Russ said, "Maybe we'll take you to see him."

"That'll be too late," Horton said. "If you take that gun away from the house, it's no good. The cops will tear this place apart looking for it. Then if we plant it back here later, they'll know it's a plant. It has to be found here now to make the rap against Velda stick."

Velda and Joey came back into the room. Joey still carried his forty-five in his hand. A sagging bulge in his coat pocket indicated where the murder gun was.

Joey said, "Let's get out of here before the cops arrive."

Russ said, "This guy's got a pretty good argument, Joey. Maybe we ought to check with Tony by phone."

Joey's eyes glittered with such sudden deadliness that Russ took an involuntary step backward. "You're running things, Joey," he said hurriedly. "It was just a suggestion."

Joey said in a quiet tone of finality, "This guy's a con artist. He's always got a good argument. We'll do it the way Tony said." He shifted his gaze to Hippo. "You got some suggestions too?"

His tone made it a challenge. Hippo said, "I didn't say nothing."

"Then let's get moving," Joey snapped.

Looking at Velda, Russ said, "We just gonna walk off and leave her?"

"She won't talk," Joey told him, gesturing Horton toward the hall. "She can't afford to."

Horton said helpfully, "Maybe you'd better check that with Tony."

Joey gave him a shove toward the door.

Russ said in a loud voice, "Listen, Joey. You're running this show. But I don't like the idea of leaving a witness around who can testify that we took this guy for a ride. What can we lose by taking her to see Tony?"

Joey's only real goal was to kill Horton. He was obsessed with the thought of vengeance to the point where nothing else really mattered to him. He said with a mixture of impatience and indifference, "Bring her along, if you want. But start moving."

When Velda started to open her mouth to register a protest, Joey suddenly let his eyes glitter at her. "I've got a short fuse," he told her. "You say one word and I'll put a bullet through your head. Move!"

Velda scurried after Horton without emitting a sound.

Until they reached the Oldsmobile, Horton didn't give up hope that the police might still arrive in time to rescue them. But not a soul was in sight as they went down the front walk and across the street. For all the sign of life from the houses either side of Velda's, they might have been vacant. With a touch of bitterness it occurred to Horton that the only time in his life he actually looked forward to the arrival of police, they had failed him.

Velda was ordered to sit next to Hippo in the front seat of the Olds. Horton drew the center of the back seat, between Russ and Joey.

Hippo drove right past the parked Ford in which Belle sat waiting. Her gaze met Horton's as they passed, but aside from a slight widening of her eyes, she gave no indication of surprise. He controlled an urge to turn and glance through the rear window to see if she was swinging the Ford around to follow.

Hippo headed straight for the Sixth Ward Athletic Club. He parked the Olds in the alley behind it, and they all entered the building by a rear door. A set of back stairs took them to the second floor without being observed. When they reached the same small office where Horton had been taken before, Joey left the two prisoners under the guns of Russ and Hippo and went off to find Tony Manzetti.

Horton dropped into a chair against the wall and calmly lit a cigarette. After a moment of indecision, Velda sat next to him and gave him a tentative smile.

"Want to be friends again, huh?" Horton asked with irony.

He offered a cigarette and lit it for her. Under cover of leaning toward him for the light, she asked in a low voice, "What will they do with us?"

Before Horton could reply, Russ said, "All right, break it up. Either of you have anything to say, speak up so we can all hear."

Then the office door opened and Tony Manzetti came in followed by Joey.

CHAPTER XXVI

The racketeer looked at Horton with satisfaction. After a brief glance at Velda, he ignored her.

In a jovial tone he said to Horton, "You've given me a little trouble, Jimmy-boy. What'd you do with my Buick and with Russ's gun?"

"The Buick's on Quincy's Used-Car Lot," Horton said. "Unless one of the salesmen has sold it."

"Yeah? No wonder we couldn't find it. My boys have been checking the streets. How about the gun?"

"Russ seems to have acquired another," Horton said. "He doesn't need it."

Manzetti laughed. "We got lots of guns," he agreed. "We'll skip it." He glanced at Velda to include her in the conversation. "You kids shouldn't have picked me as your patsy. Now see the jam you're in?"

Horton blew a smoke ring and examined it with mild pride as it floated away. "Joey obviously hasn't told you the whole story, Manzetti. He's given you a lot of unnecessary trouble just because he's after my hide. I had things all set up to take both of us off the spot when he blundered in and complicated everything again."

Joey started to say, "This smooth-talking—" when Manzetti silenced him with a gesture.

"Go on, Jimmy-boy," he invited pleasantly.

"That gun in Joey's side pocket is the one that killed Quincy. I had a comparison test run on it. It was—"

"How'd you manage that?" Manzetti interrupted.

"You're not the only one with a contact at Police Headquarters. How I worked it isn't important, but there isn't any question about it being the murder gun. It was Quincy's gun, and probably is registered to him. It was safely planted in a dresser drawer at Velda's house, and police were on their way to search for it. If they'd found it, it would have been all the evidence the police needed to drop the murder in her lap. They wouldn't even have glanced in your direction. But Joey's got a grudge. He doesn't care how much trouble he causes you, so long as he draws the privilege of killing me."

Manzetti's jovial smile had faded as Horton spoke. He turned his head to study his number-one hatchet man. "Is this true, Joey?" he asked quietly.

In a sullen voice Joey said, "You can't believe anything this guy says, Boss."

Manzetti glanced at Russ. "How about this, Russ?"

With an uncomfortable look at Joey, Russ said, "Well, Horton told the same story before we hauled him and the dame away from her house."

Manzetti swung back toward Joey, and his eyes suddenly blazed. He yelled, "You give us two people to get rid of just to satisfy a personal grudge? Who the hell you think you are?"

Joey's face paled, leaving the scar on his thin cheek a fiery red. His pallor wasn't fright, though. His expression resembled that of a dog whipped by its master.

"Give me that gun!" Manzetti snapped, holding out his hand.

Wordlessly Joey brought out the gun he had gotten from Velda. When Manzetti jerked it from his grasp and glared at Joey, for a breathtaking moment Horton thought he meant to shoot the thin gunman in cold blood.

Apparently Joey thought so too, for he flinched. He made not the slightest movement of defense, though. He just stood regarding his employer with a sick expression on his face.

Tension in the room relaxed when Manzetti merely dropped his gaze to the gun and studied its serial number. Wheeling around, the racketeer strode to his desk and slammed himself into the swivel chair behind it. He lifted the phone and dialed a number.

A small shudder passed over Joey's body and his shoulders slumped as tension drained out of him.

Manzetti said into the phone, "Let me talk to Sergeant Thom."

After a pause, he said, "Tony Manzetti, Sergeant. See if this gun is registered, will you?" He read off its serial number.

There was a wait of a minute or two, then Manzetti said, "Yeah? Okay, that's fine, Sergeant. Thanks. And forget this call, huh?"

Hanging up, he glared at Joey and said with barely suppressed rage, "You fixed things good. This is registered to Quincy, just like Horton said. Why the hell didn't you at least have sense enough to phone me?"

"I suggested it," Horton offered. He smiled at the uncomfortable Joey.

Manzetti blazed at Horton, "You got nothing to be happy about, Buster. You're as good as dead. Both of you."

Horton's smile faded. Velda gave Manzetti a frightened look.

"Now we've got to wind it up," Manzetti raged at Joey. "Take 'em out somewhere and rig it double. Murder and suicide, or a suicide pact—I don't care which. Just so it's foolproof. We'll settle your working off personal grudges on my time later."

He flung the gun back to Joey so hard, Joey backed a pace and grunted when he caught it.

Joey said tentatively, "The woman too, Boss? She couldn't rat on us."

"You harebrain!" Manzetti spat at him. "With the gun traced back to Quincy, you think the cops won't go to work on her? Even if you used a different gun, they'd pull her in for questioning after getting a tip that the murder gun was at her house. And if you think I'm betting on a woman being able to keep her mouth shut even to save her own skin, guess again. Do what I said."

Velda said in a panicky voice, "I wouldn't talk. Honest I wouldn't."

Manzetti didn't even bother to answer. Rising from his desk, he stalked out and slammed the door.

There was a period of silence. Finally Russ emitted a long-held breath. "Whew! I told you we should have checked by phone, Joey."

Joey had regained both his color and his aplomb, now that the only person in the world whose opinion mattered to him was out of sight.

"Shut up," he said coldly. "Let's get out of here. We can figure out where to pull it on the way."

Horton and Velda were herded down the back stairs again to the Olds parked in the alley. Seating arrangements were the same as before. Hippo drove as far as the alley mouth, then braked and looked inquiringly back at Joey.

"Take a left," Joey ordered.

As the Olds swung left, Horton saw the rented Ford parked just next to the mouth of the alley, facing it. Belle sat behind the wheel gazing into a compact mirror as she touched lipstick to her mouth. She didn't glance up as the Olds passed, but a moment later Horton heard the motor of her car start.

Following Joey's instructions, Hippo drove north clear to the edge of town. As they passed the city-line marker, Hippo asked, "Where we bound, Joey?"

"Tony's beach house," Joey said.

They drove in silence for a time. Then Russ said, "We can't pull it there."

"You think I'm that stupid?" Joey asked frigidly. "We'll just hold them there until dark."

Another mile went by in silence before Russ finally said, "I been thinking, Joey. If this is supposed to look like a suicide pact, the cops are gonna wonder how they got to wherever we dump them. There ought to be a car around that it'll look like they came in."

"I know it," Joey said in a short voice.

With a show of spirit Russ said, "Well, you gonna let us in on your plans?"

"He doesn't have any," Horton said. "He's ad libbing as he goes along."

Without a word Joey smashed the barrel of his gun across Horton's forehead. The blow rocked Horton back in the seat without knocking him out. Dazedly he raised a hand to touch his forehead. His fingers came away wet with blood from a two-inch gash.

"Go ahead and mark me up, you stupid jerk," Horton said thickly. "The cops will go fine for your rigged suicide when they see I was beaten to hell before I died."

With an enraged expression on his face Joey raised the gun to hit him again. Russ reached across Horton to grab Joey's wrist.

"Hold it, Joey!" he said sharply. "The guy's right."

The rage gradually left Joey's face. Russ released his grip on Joey's wrist and sat back.

Again there was a period of silence. Joey's eyes continued to glitter at Horton, but he made no further attempt at violence. Presently he said to Russ in a tone of near apology, "We can put the slug right in the cut. Nobody'll be able to tell the difference."

There was no more conversation the rest of the trip. Their destination was a trim, four-room beach cottage about ten miles north of town. They reached it by means of a dirt-road turnoff from the main highway which wound through underbrush for a couple of hundred yards before it ended at a sand-and-shale strip of beach at the river edge.

The cottage was well-isolated, Horton noted as they all climbed from the car. There was no other building in sight in any direction.

Except for a splitting headache, Horton had recovered from the pistol blow by the time they reached the cottage. He and Velda were ordered inside and told to take seats in a small but well-furnished front room.

"I'm going to leave you guys in charge while I drive back to town," Joey told Russ and Hippo. "I'll be back about dark. Stay on your toes for a change."

"Where you going?" Russ asked.

"To case the dame's house. The cops won't stick around there forever. If they don't leave the place staked out, that's where we'll pull it."

Russ frowned. "Ain't that taking a chance? Suppose it is staked out?"

"Then we'll figure out another plan," Joey snapped.

Russ shrugged. "You're calling the shots."

"Where would be more logical?" Joey inquired. "The cops find them both dead in her bedroom, him with a gun in his hand. He's bumped her and then himself. Makes more sense than if they was found in a ditch someplace."

He went out after a final admonition to Russ and Hippo to stay alert. They heard the Olds start and drive away.

Russ thoughtfully looked Horton and Velda over, then said to Hippo, "Why sit here with guns in our hands all day? See if you can find some rope."

Nodding, Hippo lumbered off into the kitchen. Shortly he returned with a long section of clothesline.

"On your feet," Russ ordered the prisoners.

He herded them at gunpoint into a bedroom containing a double bed.

"You first," Russ said to Horton. "Lie on your stomach and put your hands behind you."

Horton removed his hat and hung it on a bedpost. He lay face down on the bed.

While Russ held the gun, Hippo thoroughly hogtied Horton, then rolled him over with his back to the wall. After similarly tying Velda, he rolled her into a position facing Horton. Thoughtfully Hippo removed her little black hat and laid it on the dresser.

After studying his handiwork, Hippo said, "Maybe they could shift around back-to-back and pick each other's knots loose, huh?"

"That's easy to fix," Russ said.

Putting away his gun, he heaved the bed away from the wall. Going behind it, he looped a short length of clothesline around Horton's wrists, tied the other end to the sidebar on which the springs rested. After pushing the bed back to its original position against the wall, he performed a similar operation on Velda's side of the bed.

"Houdini couldn't get out of that," he said to Hippo. "Hunt up a deck. I'll take you over at a little gin."

CHAPTER XXVII

Hippo's knot-tying had been designed more for security than for the comfort of the prisoners. Their feet were awkwardly drawn up behind them and lashed to their wrists. After one brief test of the knots, Horton gave up all effort to free himself.

"Don't try to struggle," he advised Velda. "He tied them so the knots tighten if you force them any." Already he was beginning to regret his own brief attempt, for it had drawn the bonds tight enough to partially cut off circulation.

They lay with their thighs pressed together and their noses almost touching. Velda looked as though she were on the verge of tears.

"Go ahead and cry, if it will make you feel better," Horton suggested.

Velda gave her head a small shake. "I couldn't use my handkerchief," she said forlornly. "My nose would get all shiny."

Even after all his experience with women, Horton wondered if he would ever fully understand them. Trussed up like a chicken and facing imminent death, Velda was still concerned about her appearance.

Velda said in a small voice, "What are we going to do?"

"Nothing at the moment," he told her. He listened to the sound of the gin game going on in the front room. "Any idea what time it is?"

"It must be past one." Her face grew tearful again. "I'm hungry."

My God, Horton thought. First she worries about her face, and now about her stomach.

He said with heavy irony, "That's quite a serious problem. Glad I don't have any large worries."

She gave him a reproachful look. "You're making fun of me. You ought to want to co-operate. We're in this together."

"If I could think of anything to do, I'd be glad to co-operate," he said with sincerity. "What would you suggest?"

"I don't know. But at least we ought to be friends. In case we think of something."

"All right. We're friends."

"You mean it?" she asked. "You'll help me if a chance comes up, and I'll help you? We'll stick together?"

"It's a pact," he said. "A mutual defense pact."

"We won't try to throw each other to the wolves any more? Like you did me first, and then I did you?"

"It's all for one and one for all."

She moved her head an inch and kissed him on the lips. "That seals it."

"Contract is signed," he said. "But I still haven't any ideas."

Velda sighed. "I wish we weren't tied up."

Horton cocked an eyebrow at her.

"I mean at least we'd have something to do," she explained. "Would you like to kiss me again?"

The dialogue struck Horton as a little unreal.

"I'm afraid I couldn't keep my mind on sex at the moment," he said politely.

"Oh," she said a little disappointedly.

Conversation lapsed for a time. Then Velda said, "You don't still think I shot John, do you?"

"Didn't you?"

"Would I lie to you now?" she asked. "We'll both probably be dead in a few hours."

"Who did it then?"

"Manzetti must have had it done."

Horton shook his head. "I don't think so. I don't think he even sent that threat. He just wants the case wound up because he's afraid the papers will get on his back if I'm proven innocent."

"Well, I didn't do it. What I told you about the gun disappearing before the murder was true."

"Who had access to it, aside from you and your husband?" he asked.

"Nobody. Except the cleaning maid. And she'd have no reason to kill him."

"You must have had visitors in the house occasionally. Do you have any idea how long the gun had been missing?"

She thought for a moment. "Not long, I'm sure. I think I recall seeing it when I was putting laundry in John's dresser drawers a few days before he was killed. That would have been on Monday, five days before the murder."

"And it was missing Friday evening when he looked for it?"

"Yes."

Horton said musingly, "That leaves only four days during which it could have been lifted. You ought to be able to remember what guests you had during that time."

"We didn't have any," she said. "Recently we hardly ever entertained. My husband and I hadn't been getting along."

"Yeah, I know. Wasn't anyone at all in the house?"

"Well, my husband did have some people over for a business conference of some kind. On Wednesday evening, I believe. But he barely knew them. As a matter of fact, I don't believe he'd even met the man before that night. They wouldn't have had any reason to kill him."

"Who were they?"

"A Mrs. Whitney and a Major Walsh. It was something about some stocks Mrs. Whitney wanted advice on."

Horton said nothing. He was too numb to speak. He felt as though he had been hit in the pit of the stomach by a giant fist.

"I had lunch with the major just yesterday," Velda went on, unaware of the bombshell she had dropped. "He's a free lance writer doing research on the case for some magazine. I don't know what his connection with Mrs. Whitney is."

Russ's voice from the doorway said, "What's all the gab?"

Horton looked over at him, and Velda twisted her neck to look at him too. Apparently Russ didn't expect an answer to his question. He came over to the bed to examine their bonds. Satisfied that they were still secure, he returned to the front room.

"It's your deal," they heard him say to Hippo.

The rest of the afternoon dragged by slowly. Finding Horton suddenly and unaccountably withdrawn, Velda finally gave up attempts to keep the conversation alive and dropped off to sleep. Beyond periodic checks by Russ or Hippo to make sure the bonds were still holding, there were no interruptions to Horton's thoughts.

It was hard for him to accept the implications of Velda's story. But he had no choice. Belle had not only failed to mention her visit to Quincy's home, she had stated in answer to Horton's direct question that her only contact with Quincy had been a casual meeting in the Hotel Lawford bar.

What had happened between the Wednesday night meeting at Quincy's home and the Saturday morning the man died, he wondered? Had Quincy discovered he was being conned? And had either Belle or the colonel taken extreme measures to avoid arrest?

It seemed incredible that either of them would kill for such a reason. Why not just flee town? And why had Quincy taken no action if he knew they were a confidence team? Why hadn't he had them thrown into jail?

There must have been some factor other than simple detection of the con game, Horton decided. Perhaps instead of calling the police, Quincy used his knowledge as a lever to force Belle and the colonel to do something they didn't want to do. Something so repugnant to them that they killed him to avoid it.

What, he wondered? A possibility occurred to him. Belle was an extremely attractive woman. And Quincy had been on the verge of divorce from his wife. Had he taken the opportunity to play wolf? Perhaps issued an ultimatum to Belle that she could either play ball or go to jail?

That might be enough to bring her to murder. Or, considering the colonel's chivalrous nature, it might be enough to make him kill in defense of her honor.

Horton couldn't imagine any lesser motive that could bring either to the point of taking a human life.

He was tempted to awaken Velda and ask her opinion as to whether or not her husband had been capable of that type of lecherous blackmail. Then he decided it would involve too much explanation, and that the motive wasn't important anyway.

Whatever the motive, the facts seemed inescapable.

Everything began to fit into place. Even the mysterious visitor who had been leaving Velda's house by the back door as he entered the front. Belle, no doubt, returning the gun just in time for him to find it.

She wouldn't have bothered, he thought, if he hadn't accidentally been accused of the murder. He had no doubt that she was sincerely in love with him. She had done everything possible to help him prove his innocence. Even to framing Velda for the crime.

Apparently the original plan had been to let Tony Manzetti take the blame. The threatening note could have had no other purpose. Probably the gun had been stolen from Quincy's house on the spur of the moment, simply because it was available and neither Belle nor the colonel owned any other. Confidence people rarely possessed guns. If Horton hadn't been caught in the trap by coincidence, the gun probably would now be in the river. But with Horton in danger, the plan had been changed. The gun was returned to throw the blame on Velda.

Horton experienced no lift of accomplishment from having figured things out. He had never felt so miserable in his life.

CHAPTER XXVIII

Horton guessed that at least four hours had passed when he heard the sound of a car approaching the cottage along the dirt lane leading from the highway. The sound awakened Velda.

"Is that Joey returning already?" she asked fearfully.

"Probably," he said. "It must be past five."

In the other room they heard footsteps move unhurriedly to the front door. Then Russ's tense voice said, "Hey, Hippo! It's not Joey. It's some dame."

There was the sound of Hippo lumbering over to the door to have a look too.

"All alone," they heard Hippo say. "Better see what she wants and get rid of her."

The screen door creaked open and slammed again. Then, from outside, Belle's voice came clearly. "Is this the Winthrop place?"

Russ's reply was too low-toned for Horton to understand.

"They said the first turnoff after the Texaco station," Belle's voice said.

The screen door opened and slammed again. From the front porch Hippo called, "This is the second turnoff, lady. You missed it."

A sound from the bedroom window turned Horton's eyes that way. The insert screen in the lower part of the window was being quietly lifted out by someone outside. Then the window was silently pushed all the way up and a shapely leg hooked over the sill.

Horton's eyes bugged in astonishment as Helen stepped into the room. She had a thirty-eight revolver in her hand.

Touching a finger to her lips in a gesture of silence, Helen climbed over the foot of the bed, straddled Horton's legs and began to tug at his knots with her free hand. When they didn't give, she dropped the gun on the bed between Horton and Velda and tugged with both hands.

Outside Belle was saying, "It's the next turn back, then? It must be hard to see, or I wouldn't have missed it. Is there any landmark?"

One knot gave, but it was only the one lashing his wrists to the side-bar. Horton shifted himself face down so that Helen could get at the other knots more easily.

Russ's voice said something they couldn't catch. Hippo called, "Why don't you go back to the Texaco station and start over, lady?"

Suddenly Horton felt his bonds loosen. Helen reeled in several feet of rope, scrambled off the bed and tossed the rope on the floor. Horton let his legs flop full-length on the bed, got his hands beneath his chest and tried to push himself to his knees. Both hands were numb and there was no strength in his arms.

Velda grunted as he rolled over half on top of her and managed to struggle to a sitting position. He rolled the rest of the way across her, dropped his feet to the floor and pushed himself erect.

His legs were numb, too. His knees crumpled and he fell heavily to the floor.

The sound of his fall seemed enormous to all of them. With a frightened look at the door, Helen rushed to kneel over him. Frantically she began massaging his arms.

It seemed to Horton that minutes dragged by before he felt the tingling of restored circulation begin.

Pushing Helen away, he beat at his legs with both hands until they started to tingle too. The exercise completed restoring circulation to his arms, so that when he finally got to his feet, he had full use of them. His legs were still half asleep, but at least he could walk at a wobbling gait.

Just as the screen door opened and slammed again, Horton reached across Velda and grabbed up the gun Helen had dropped on the bed. When he motioned Helen back out of sight of the bedroom door, she pressed herself against the wall at the foot of the bed. Horton wobbled over to take up a position alongside the door.

Apparently Hippo meant to make one of his periodic checks of the prisoners. His ponderous footsteps moved straight from the front door toward the bedroom. He walked right past Horton and came to a startled halt when he spotted Helen against the wall.

Raising his gun, Horton brought it down squarely on top of the fat man's head. Without a sound Hippo slumped to the floor.

Moving on still unsteady legs, Horton lurched through the bedroom door and across the front room. He heard Belle's car start and back up just as he crouched beside the screen door. As the car drove off, Russ's footsteps sounded on the porch.

He, too, walked right past Horton. An instant later he was sprawled face-down on the floor, unconscious.

Helen appeared in the bedroom doorway. She looked at Horton with a mixture of relief and concern.

"What happened to your poor forehead?" she asked.

"I tried to bend a gun barrel with it. It's all right. Where the devil did you come from?"

Before answering, Helen moved forward into his arms and kissed him.

Then she said, "Your friend Belle brought me. She couldn't find anyone else to help her. When she told me what trouble you were in, I got someone to take over the desk and came with her.

"I have to signal Belle," she added, and withdrew from his arms and stepped out on the front porch.

Through the screen Horton saw her wave her arms in an all-clear signal. A moment later he heard the sound of Belle's car returning.

When Helen came back inside again, her body had begun to tremble in delayed reaction. Concerned, Horton thrust his gun into a hip pocket, took her in his arms and held her for a moment.

"I'll be all right in a minute," she said. "I was so scared, Jim. If it hadn't been you tied up, I never could have done it."

She shook herself and the trembling passed. Horton gave her shoulder a reassuring pat and turned toward the door. As he pulled open the screen door, he said over his shoulder, "If you're up to it, go untie Velda."

Helen frowned. She made no move toward the bedroom.

Horton was on the porch then, and had let the screen door close behind him. "Go ahead," he said through the screen. "We don't have much time."

Then he turned his attention forward as Belle stopped the rented car in front of the cottage.

"Pull it around back and out of sight," he called to her. "In case the other guy comes back before we get out of here."

Belle nodded, backed the car and drove it around to the other side of the cottage, where it couldn't be seen by anyone driving down the dirt lane. Horton went back inside to find Helen standing where he had left her.

"What's the matter?" he asked her.

"I wouldn't touch that murderess," Helen said with an expression of distaste. "She can stay tied up as far as I'm concerned."

"She didn't kill him," Horton told her.

He moved past her into the bedroom, stepped over the prone Hippo and bent to loosen Velda's knots. By the time Belle came into the house, Velda was sitting up massaging her arms and legs. Helen had come as far as the bedroom doorway, and Velda looked up to give her a brief glance.

Helen swung her back and marched into the front room.

Helping Velda erect, Horton supported her into the other room and over to a sofa. Velda sat and resumed her massaging. She didn't look at Helen, and Helen didn't look at her.

Belle said in a concerned voice, "What happened to your head, Jim?"

"Bumped it," Horton said briefly.

"Oh? How did you like our U.S. Cavalry act?"

"Fine," Horton said, not meeting her eyes. He couldn't at the moment, after the thoughts he had wrestled with while trussed to the bed.

Belle gave him a puzzled look. To cover his feelings, Horton said in a brisk tone, "Let's get these characters tied up. You can tell me how you happened to make like the cavalry while we're working."

Velda was not yet in shape to assist. She remained on the sofa massaging circulation back into her limbs while the other three went to the bedroom. Together they managed to heave Hippo's dead weight onto the bed.

It gave Horton some satisfaction to hogtie the fat man in exactly the way Hippo had tied him. After rolling him over against the wall, they carried the lighter figure of Russ from the front room, tossed him on the bed and trussed him up, too.

As they worked, Belle explained how she and Helen happened to join forces as a rescue team.

"I followed you to the Sixth Ward Athletic Club," she said. "And then clear out here. When that third man drove back toward town alone, leaving you and his two companions here, I figured you wouldn't be moving again for a while, and I'd have time to get help. I was afraid to call the police. I assumed your plan to plant the gun at Velda's had misfired, or Manzetti's men wouldn't have kidnaped you. I thought bringing in the police would just put you from the frying pan into the fire.

"I wasn't thinking too clearly, I guess. I was nearly crazy with worry. Instead of finding a phone, I drove clear to the Rafferty House. I don't think I dropped below eighty all the way, even inside the city. The colonel wasn't in and had left no word as to where he was. I left a note in his box explaining the situation, then drove over to the Lawford. I had the wild idea of getting the gun you had left with me and coming back here to rescue you alone. Then, after I'd gotten it from my room and had come back downstairs again, I spotted Helen on the desk. I thought that if she was as crazy about you as you are about her, she ought to be willing to help. So I walked up to the desk and told her the whole thing."

Helen looked at Horton and blushed. "I nearly went into hysterics," she said. "Belle was already near hysterics, so my reaction didn't help things much. But we calmed each other down during the ride out here."

"We should have worked out our strategy on the way here too," Belle said. "But we were both too upset even to start thinking about what we intended to do until we got here. We've been around here for hours, peeking in windows to locate where you were and where Manzetti's men were. Helen finally thought of the plan of me luring them out front while she sneaked in the bedroom window."

Horton pulled the last knot tight just as Belle finished her story. As he straightened, the sound of a car coming down the dirt lane reached them.

Gesturing to the two women to stay in the bedroom, Horton crossed the front room with long strides and peered through the screen door. The gray Oldsmobile was just pulling to a halt outside.

"Get in the bedroom with the others," he whispered to Velda. "And stay out of sight. Joey's back and he's got Tony Manzetti with him."

As Velda rose from the sofa and scurried into the bedroom, Horton flattened himself against the wall next to the front door.

CHAPTER XXIX

Two car doors slammed and two sets of footsteps approached the house. Manzetti's voice indicated that he was still in a bad mood, but that his rage had now faded to mere exasperation.

"Always, I end up doing things myself," he complained. "You might have known Velda's place would be staked out after that tip the cops got about the gun. But when you can't set it up there, you got no more ideas. You got to run back to me."

Joey said sullenly, "You hired me for my gun, not my brains."

"That's for sure," Manzetti snapped.

Feet crossed the porch and the screen door jerked open. Manzetti stalked into the room with Joey trailing him. Neither saw Horton next to the door.

"Get 'em high," Horton ordered, covering their backs with his gun.

Both men whirled. Joey's right hand streaked for his armpit in the fastest blur of motion Horton had ever seen. His gun was clear of the holster and swinging toward Horton before Horton's brain could send the message to his finger to squeeze the trigger. Horton's gun went off only a split second before the forty-five.

It was enough. Horton's slug caught Joey high in the right arm, spinning him around and making him release his gun so that it skidded across the floor beneath the edge of the sofa. Joey's bullet shattered the window next to Horton.

Manzetti's arms shot skyward when Horton swung the gun at him.

"Don't shoot!" he said in a croaking voice.

Horton glanced at Joey, who clutched at his right arm and staggered to an easy chair. Sinking into it heavily, he stared at Horton from eyes blank with shock.

Keeping Manzetti covered, Horton sidled around him to the sofa, kneeled and felt for Joey's gun. He flicked on the safety and dropped it into his pocket. Then he rose, ordered Manzetti to turn his back, and carefully frisked him.

Apparently Manzetti believed in letting the hired help do his gun work. He wasn't armed.

Horton returned his attention to Joey. The thin gunman only looked at him dully as Horton lifted the pistol Velda had given him from his pocket. Horton thrust it into his belt.

"All right, girls," he called.

Manzetti's lower jaw sagged in astonishment as three beautiful women filed from the bedroom. First in line was the brunette Belle, then the blonde Velda and, finally, the redheaded Helen.

"You sure like variety, Jimmy-boy," Manzetti finally managed in an attempt at sang-froid.

The screen door creaked open again. Horton started to turn, then froze when he found himself staring at a leveled Police Positive.

The tall, carelessly-dressed man with the gun stepped the rest of the way inside and said quietly, "Drop it, Horton. Fast."

Horton had never seen the man before, but he recognized the deep voice. It was Lieutenant Grady of Homicide. Opening his fingers, he let his gun fall to the floor.

"I didn't hear you drive up," Horton said a little stupidly.

"We didn't," Grady said in a pleasant tone. "We parked on the highway and moved in on foot."

He saw Manzetti then, and seemed a little taken aback. "Oh, hello, Mr. Manzetti."

"How are you, Lieutenant?" Manzetti asked sourly.

Grady moved forward, lifted the gun from Horton's belt, patted his pockets and took Joey's forty-five from one.

"My, my," he said. "Expecting a war?" He ran his gaze over the three women and Joey. "Quite an assemblage you have here."

A voice from the bedroom doorway said, "Couple of more in here, Lieutenant. All tied up, and they look like they're out cold."

Everyone looked that way to see a uniformed policeman standing in the doorway. He, too, had a gun in his hand.

"Check the other two rooms," Grady told him.

When the rest of the cottage had been checked without turning anyone else up, Grady said to the uniformed officer, "Guess everything's under control." He nodded toward the wounded Joey. "Better take him out to the car and put a temporary bandage on that wound. And tell Major Walsh he can come in."

Taking Joey by his good arm, the officer drew him to his feet and led him outdoors. A few moments later Colonel Bob opened the screen door and came in.

"Well, well, looks like the beachhead has been secured," he said, beaming at Grady. Then he gave Belle an apologetic smile. "When I found your note, I thought it best to bring in the police. Only good tactics to call for reinforcements when you face a superior force. Hope I didn't make a strategical error."

Belle said, "I don't know. You'll have to ask Jim."

Horton said, "It's just as well. Save going to them. Lieutenant, you want Quincy's murderer?"

Grady looked him up and down. "Thought I had him. You."

"Afraid not," Horton said. "And I can prove it, if you give me a chance."

"Go ahead," the lieutenant said agreeably.

"That gun you took out of my belt," Horton said. "That's the murder weapon. The colonel—I mean the major—already has had you check a slug from it."

"And you had it on you," Grady said. "That makes you innocent?"

"You'll find it's registered to Quincy," Horton told him. "I couldn't possibly have had access to it. It disappeared from Quincy's house a few days before the murder, and was put back again yesterday. In an attempt to frame Quincy's wife. But that was an after-thought. I think it was taken originally simply because the killer didn't know where else to get a gun. The plan was to frame Manzetti by sending that threatening note just before the murder. But the killer was kind of fond of me. When I got accused of the murder, the plan was changed to frame Velda."

"Sounds complicated," Grady said. "Can you prove it?"

Horton turned to Belle. In a heavy voice he said, "Why didn't you tell me you visited Quincy's home last Wednesday night, Belle?"

Belle's eyes widened. "Because I didn't."

"Velda says you did."

Belle glanced at Velda. "She's mistaken. The col— the major and I did have an appointment to see him, but we broke it. I told you why."

Horton glanced at Velda. She shrugged. "John told me they were coming. I assumed they kept the engagement."

"You mean you weren't there?"

"I went out that night. These people meant nothing to me. It was just a business meeting."

Horton's mind staggered under a sudden mixture of emotions. The surge of joy he felt that neither the colonel nor Belle were killers was followed by consternation as his case abruptly crashed about his ears. Through a mental fog he heard Belle saying, "What are you getting at, Jim?"

"Nothing," he managed to say, trying to re-organize his thoughts. Doggedly he went on, "Someone stole the gun with the deliberate idea of killing Quincy."

"Who?" Grady asked.

Horton was silent. So was everyone else, waiting for him to speak.

Helen broke the silence. "It was Velda!"

Everyone looked at Velda.

"That's a lie!" Velda said loudly. "Until today I didn't even know John was killed by his own gun."

"Fiddlesticks," Helen said scornfully. "You're overdoing the dumb act. Even if you were innocent, you knew the gun was missing. And you knew he'd been killed by a forty-five. Are you trying to pretend you can't put two and two together?"

Grady asked curiously, "How would she know it was a forty-five?"

"It was in the papers," Helen said.

Grady shook his head. "We didn't release any information about the weapon. All the papers said was that he was shot."

A tingle went along Horton's spine. He stared at Helen as a monstrous thought formed in his mind.

"Helen," he said slowly. "It was you who suggested that Quincy's gun might have been the murder weapon. I knew it was a forty-five because Major Walsh told me. And he got the information from the police. *But how did you know?*"

"Don't be silly," she said, coloring. "You're mistaken. I never said what it was."

"Yes, you did," Horton said, taking a step toward her. "I remember your exact words. 'Wasn't the murder gun a forty-five automatic?' You even knew it was an automatic. I remember telling you it was a forty-five, but there was no way to tell whether it was an automatic or a revolver from the slug."

"You're wrong," she said, staring at him white-faced. "You're not remembering it right."

Horton took another step toward her. "Yes, I am. And you had access to the gun. You still had your keys to the house. You only gave me the front door key, and kept the back door key to put back the gun. It was you who left by the back door just as I came in the front. You were away from the hotel when your step-father was killed, too. I met you coming back right after the murder. You hadn't been to lunch. You'd been down to Quincy's Used-Car Lot."

Helen pressed her hands to her cheeks. "Don't say that!" she said breathlessly. "Don't I mean anything to you?"

Horton closed his eyes for a moment. When he opened them again, he said in a dead voice, "Not if you're a killer."

Her face crumpled. "It was for you," she said. "Don't you see? I could just have thrown the gun away, and nobody would ever have suspected. I put it back to protect you. I even risked my life to save you out here. How can you do this to me?"

He looked at her for a moment with deep pain in his eyes. Then he sighed and turned away.

"Is that enough for you, Lieutenant?" he asked dully. "Am I still charged with anything?"

Helen had collapsed into the chair vacated by Joey and had dropped her face into her hands. The lieutenant glanced at her and then, a little uncomfortably, at Manzetti.

"I guess you're cleared, Horton," he said. "But there's still the matter of what was happening out here. I haven't had an explanation of that yet."

"I don't want to press any charges," Horton said. "Call it a wild party that got out of hand." He looked steadily at Manzetti. "Mr. Manzetti will explain it to you."

Grady said in a tone of relief, "Well, if everybody concerned is satisfied, I don't see any point—"

"I didn't say I was satisfied," Horton interrupted. "I just said I didn't want to press charges. There's one small item to clean up."

Walking over to Manzetti, he said, "I got two bumps on the head on account of you, Tony-boy." He touched the clotted gash on his forehead. "One here, one around back. You figure we're even?"

"Sure, Jimmy-boy," Manzetti said heartily.

"I don't," Horton told him. "I figure I still owe you something."

"Yeah?" Manzetti said less heartily. "What?"

"This," Horton said, uncorking a fast right cross that lifted the racketeer's feet six inches from the floor and laid him full-length on the sofa.

"Let's go back to town," Horton said to Belle.

CHAPTER XXX

By noon the next day Horton had obtained his impounded Mercury from the Police Department, his suitcase from the Palais Royal, and had closed out his account at the Rice City National Bank. After settling his delinquent bill at the Hotel Lawford, he checked back in. He asked for and got the room adjoining Belle's.

Belle accompanied him while he attended to all this business. If she suspected that at one point of the proceedings Horton had been on the verge of accusing her of the murder, she tactfully didn't mention it. Horton didn't mention it either. They had too many more important things to talk about.

Brooding about the emotions he had felt during the period he thought he was falling in love with Helen, Horton came to the conclusion that his uncomfortable feeling about Belle had deeper significance than mere guilt. Since he'd never before felt guilty about breaking off with a woman, he decided Belle must be more important to him than he'd suspected, and his temporary infatuation for Helen had simply blinded him to the fact.

He was considerably surprised when after explaining this self-analysis to Belle, she didn't immediately swoon into his arms.

After contemplating him moodily, she said, "It's just rebound, my love. Let's sit it out for a while."

"What do you mean, rebound?" he asked.

"You wouldn't understand," she told him. "You've never been in love before. Any teen-age boy could tell you that after a disappointment in love, you're ripe to fall again for the nearest available female. You've just never had the experience."

"I thought you said you loved me," he said a little sulkily.

"Oh, I do," she assured him. "But I don't want to spend the rest of my life thinking I trapped you when your defenses were down. Come around again when you're sure you're over Helen."

"I am over Helen," he insisted. "And what do you mean, 'Come around?' I'm not planning to let you out of my sight."

She gave him a gentle smile. "You'll have to, I'm afraid. As soon as the colonel and I finish our business with Mr. Tyrell, we'll be leaving town."

"Let him leave alone," Horton said. "At least we could be business partners."

"And break your rule about always working alone?" she asked with raised brows.

"Come off it, Belle," he said impatiently. "You've put me in my place. You don't have to drive it into the ground. What do you want? To be begged?"

"Of course not." She considered the idea with growing enthusiasm. "We would make quite a team. I'm really more your type of woman than Helen was. Aside from a propensity for homicide, she was much too moral for you."

"How will the colonel take your leaving him?" Horton asked.

"In stride. He's quite self-sufficient, you know. He'll probably be breaking in a new assistant within twenty-four hours."

By prearrangement they met the colonel for lunch at the Rafferty House. Colonel Bob examined Belle's glowing face with an air of resignation as they approached the table he had reserved.

Rising, he said, "I detect a certain air about you people. Is there something you want to ask me, young man?"

Horton held a chair for Belle, waited until he and the colonel were both seated, then cocked an eyebrow at Colonel Bob. "Like what?" he asked.

Belle said, "The colonel thinks he's my father. He wants to know your intentions."

"Oh," Horton said. He glanced sidewise at Belle.

"I don't think he has any intentions," Belle said. "He's still recovering from a broken heart." She turned to Horton. "I was just being a gracious loser, Jim. But now I can tell you the truth. She really does dye her hair."

A waiter interrupted the conversation to take their orders.

When they had all ordered and the waiter had moved away again, Colonel Bob said, "Something I still don't get. I understand Helen's motive. She resented being chucked out of Quincy's house and having her allowance cut off because of her objection to his second marriage. And she rightly figured she was still in his will, so she'd get at least something when he died. But if she hated Velda so, why didn't she try to frame her from the beginning instead of Manzetti?"

"She didn't know Velda had any motive for wanting him dead," Horton said. "The gossip about Velda had never reached her. As far as she knew, Quincy was living a life of marital bliss. The minute she found out from me that Velda did have a motive, she tried fast enough to frame her."

"Then it wasn't just regard for you that made her switch her plan?"

Horton looked uncomfortable. Belle came to his rescue by saying, "Partly, I think. She was concerned enough about him when I told her Manzetti's men had him captive." She smiled at Horton. "She really wasn't your type, though, even if she hadn't been a murderess, darling. She wanted to reform you."

Colonel Bob raised one eyebrow. "Darling, is it? Sure you don't wish to speak to me, young man?"

"Yes, as a matter of fact," Horton said with mock seriousness. He looked at Belle. "We may as well break it now."

Belle said, "Nothing as serious as marriage, Colonel. He wants my hand in business partnership. Will you mind losing me?"

Colonel Bob fingered his ragged mustache. "Hmm. I thought you always played lone wolf, Jim."

"Belle put it badly," Horton said. "She means we're not planning immediate marriage. She thinks I need a recovery period from Helen. It's her idea, not mine."

"Oh. So pending recovery, you're planning to work as a business team?"

Belle said, "We thought we'd try the game Jim started to pull here in a place or two. See how we get along before we take the final step."

"Hmm," the colonel said again. "I hate to lose you, Belle. But if I have to, I'd rather it would be Jim's way. Why don't you marry the man?"

"Not until I'm sure he's over his redhead," Belle said firmly.

"Well, that's your business, of course," the colonel said. "How about our pending deal?"

"Tyrell? Why don't we line him up for tomorrow night and finish it off?"

Colonel Bob nodded. "We'll all be wanting to leave town rather suddenly afterward. And I'd like to offer you young people a farewell party. Will you meet me for dinner here again tonight? Say about eight?"

Horton glanced at Belle and she nodded agreement.

"Suits us," Horton said. "Nice of you to want to."

Promptly at eight, Horton and Belle re-entered the Rafferty House dining room. Looking around, they failed to spot the colonel. They waited until the headwaiter came forward.

"Major Walsh's table, please," Horton said.

"Oh, yes," the headwaiter said politely. "You're Mr. Horton and Mrs. Whitney?"

"Yes."

The headwaiter brought a sealed envelope from his breast pocket. "The major asked me to express his apologies and give you this."

Horton and Belle retreated to the lobby to tear open the envelope. It contained a note in the colonel's flowing handwriting. The note read:

Dear children:

I leave you a parting present—a good-luck sendoff gift for your new business venture, or a wedding gift, whichever the case may be. My gift is a bit of advice for your future guidance. To wit: Never trust anyone.

As compensation for losing my partner in crime, I felt it only fair that I should have some financial gain. Mr. Tyrell parted with ten thousand dollars this afternoon. It, and I, are now on a train headed far from Rice City.

I would advise similar hasty departure on your part, Belle, as by morning it may occur to Mr. Tyrell to show his stock certificates to a broker. Jim, of course, is entirely in the clear on this, but I assume he will be concerned with your welfare.

My blessings on you both.

Robert Desmond
Colonel
U.S. Army (Ret.)

Horton and Belle looked at each other. Belle was the first to laugh.

"Why, the old crook," she said. "After all our years of partnership. He'd cheat his own mother."

Horton said, "I don't think we'd better stop for dinner. We'd better get back to the Lawford and check out. We can be three hundred miles from here by morning, if we drive all night."

Hand in hand they hurried toward the door.

www.ingramcontent.com/pod-product-compliance
Lightning Source LLC
Chambersburg PA
CBHW050759250626
47155CB00005B/2134